ALWAYS ANIKA

KELSIE STELTING

This is a work of fiction. Names, characters,
businesses, places, events and incidents are either the products of the
author's imagination or used
in a fictitious manner. Any resemblance to
actual persons, living or dead, or actual
events is purely coincidental.

An early version of this story was posted in installments on a creative forum
which is no longer active. All work is my own.

Edited by Melanie Bergeron and Theresa M. Cole.

For questions, comments, and corrections, address kelsie@kelsiestelting.com

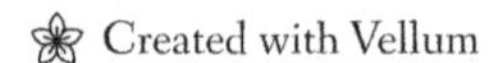

For a sweet little Papillon named Papi. You did more for me than you'll ever know.

CONTENTS

Chapter 1	1
Chapter 2	6
Chapter 3	9
Chapter 4	11
Chapter 5	14
Chapter 6	18
Chapter 7	22
Chapter 8	25
Chapter 9	28
Chapter 10	31
Chapter 11	34
Chapter 12	37
Chapter 13	40
Chapter 14	43
Chapter 15	46
Chapter 16	53
Chapter 17	55
Chapter 18	58
Chapter 19	62
Chapter 20	64
Chapter 21	68
Chapter 22	74
Chapter 23	77
Chapter 24	94
Chapter 25	100
Chapter 26	107
Chapter 27	112
Chapter 28	116
Chapter 29	120
Chapter 30	122
CHASING SKYE	125

Keep Reading 135
Also by Kelsie Stelting 137
Acknowledgments 139
Author's Note 141
About the Author 143

CHAPTER ONE

"OKAY," Miss B. began once the bell rang. "We're going to start a pen pal program this semester. Your principal thinks it will be a good idea."

The class let out a collective groan. My friend, Brandon, leaned forward and whispered in my ear.

"You know what's a good idea?" he asked. "Making out with me. You know you want to."

I rolled my eyes at him. "Just about as much as I'd like to chew glass."

"On your desk is the name and address of a soldier from Texas who is currently serving overseas. You'll write them back and forth for the rest of the semester. You must reply to their letters within one week of receiving them, and it will count as fifteen percent of your English grade," she informed us. Melissa raised her hand, and without waiting for her question, Miss B. said, "Yes, I know that means some of you will be writing more than others. You can write your letters during journaling time."

Melissa put her hand down.

"Now take out a pencil and paper, and I want a one-page, double-spaced letter, and no, you can't write really big to take up space. I'm talking to you, Brandon," she said with a smile. "I'll be reading your first letters to check for quality and length, but I'm going to give each of you a permission slip to have your parents sign saying whether or not I need to review them for the rest of the semester. Okay, get started!"

The classroom became noisy with backpack zippers and ripping paper.

"Hey, Anika," Bran whispered. "Got a piece of paper?"

I passed him one and we began writing.

Dear Shawn,

My name is Anika Anders. I'm a senior at Roderdale High School in Roderdale, Texas. Or you could call it the middle of nowhere. Either works. Really. The only things in Roderdale are a gas station, a grain elevator, a post office, and a hair salon that's only open three days a week.

My family owns a small ranch outside of town, so I usually spend my weekends working there. I'm not really sure what else I should tell you about myself. The last time I had a pen pal I was in third grade and I'm pretty sure a conversation about favorite colors/foods/hobbies was involved. (Blue. Ribs. Volleyball.)

So, tell me about yourself. Where are you from? What's your favorite color? Are you safe where you're stationed?
I also want to thank you for your service. It's very brave of you to risk your life for your country and for people you don't even know.

Always,
Anika

Within two weeks, I got a letter back. It wasn't nearly as long as mine was, but he'd enclosed a picture. Shawn looked ageless; he was somehow youthful and fun but hard and masculine at the same time. He had dark blue eyes laced with green and framed by abnormally dark lashes. His dark brown hair contrasted skin so fair it almost looked porcelain. A crooked grin turned the corners of his mouth up to reveal straight white teeth. He was in uniform, seated in front of an American flag.

Dear Anika,

My name is Shawn Adams and I'm 19 years old. I come from a town in southeast Texas about like Roderdale. Very small, but very close-knit. I appreciate it more now that I'm away. My favorite color is green. Good call on the ribs.

I can't tell you too many specifics about where I'm stationed, but as to your other question, yes, I'm about as safe as I can be in a war zone. I work as a mechanic, so it's a lot of behind-the-scenes work. I've been shot at before, but luckily, I wasn't injured... I guess I have God on my side. Sorry my reply isn't longer. I look forward to hearing from you, Anika.

Yours,
Shawn

. . .

Since he'd decided to send a picture of him I thought I should send one too. It took me a while to choose which of my senior pictures to give him, but I ended up picking one of me standing in a field close to sunset in one of my favorite dresses I never got to wear.

I studied the picture before I put it into the envelope. My usually brown hair had little bits of red in it from the sun, and my skin was nicely tanned from working outside over the summer. I wished I was thinner and that I didn't have a small chip in my front tooth from a cattle-working accident. Then I wondered why it mattered what picture I sent him.

Dear Shawn,

It's nice to "meet" you. I understand about you not being able to write more—I'm really busy, and I'm just in high school. I go out for volleyball, basketball, and track, but so does just about everyone else because our school's so small we need all the help we can get. If I'm not playing sports or working, I'm usually hanging out with my friends. I have a few close friends, but the closest ones are Leslie and Brandon. Leslie's really nice and is the most enthusiastic person I know. She gets excited about literally everything. Brandon is hilarious. He cracks me up and is always flirting with me—in a joking way. It's kind of his hobby. I don't think my dad likes it that much, though!

I guess I'll tell you about my parents, too. Dad works on our ranch, and Mom works in real estate (not that there's a whole lot around Roderdale). We own cattle and I LOVE riding horses. I'm the oldest of three children, and all I have to say about that is... our house is never quiet. Sorry, I probably talk about myself WAY too much.

Tell me more about you. What's your family like? Who's your best friend? What's it like over there? I hope you're staying safe.

Always,
Anika

"I can't believe you actually take this seriously," Brandon told me as I carefully sealed the envelope so I could turn it in to Miss B. My parents had agreed to let me keep my privacy, so I just had to hold the letter up so she could see that I'd written enough.

I rolled my eyes at him. "It's fifteen percent of my grade."

"Are you sure it doesn't have anything to do with how sexy he is?" Leslie asked. "I wish mine was as hot as yours!"

"Me too," Brandon chimed in. "Mine's a thirty-year-old technician. What's sexy about that?"

I rolled my eyes again. "I'm looking for a good grade, not a husband."

Miss B. gave us a pointed look and told us to be quiet.

"An's in love!" Bran explained. "I need to kick some ass!"

"Brandon," Miss B. barely covered her smile, "let's leave the 'ass-kicking' for after class, shall we?"

CHAPTER TWO

Dear Anika,

I love hearing about your family. It almost makes me feel like I'm back home. I lived out in the country as well, but the only sport I played in high school was football—running back, if you wanted to know. I've lost touch with most of my friends from high school since I enlisted. Everyone's busy with college and family and girls and whatever else keeps them busy in life. My best friend joined with me, though, and was somehow lucky enough to be stationed in the same place I am. He's a computer genius, and I'm starting to wonder if that has anything to do with our luck. I'm definitely not complaining, though. I have two sisters, so he's like the brother I never had.

I never dreamt I would be overseas so quick. I miss America. I miss seeing trees and grass and never having to wonder if I'm going to make it to the next day or not. Most of all, I miss home. It's nice to have someone to write to about it, though.

Yours,
Shawn

Dear Shawn,

I bet it's hard. Sometimes, though, I just want to get away from this place. This guy that graduated last year, Rhett, walked up to me after a game. He had a dumb smirk on his face and said, "Wanna know how we could make everyone jealous?" and stupid me asked, "how?" and he said, "Go out with me." I didn't really say anything, but he asked again... I guess I thought if I just ignored him, he would leave me alone. I mean, I don't like him, but there's always that little (very little) part of you that wants to be the girl everyone wants to be, you know, the one that dates the stud bull rider, the cute mature guy.

There's also another (bigger) part of me that hates jerks. Still, it kind of stinks to not be dating anyone because our winter dance is coming up. It's still a few weeks away, but it kinda looks like I'll be going alone to my senior Swirl. How lovely.

But I know you're probably worse off, and I'm probably being selfish, as usual... sigh. You're definitely a hero for what you're doing.

Always,
Anika

I TURNED the letter in just as the bell rang, and Brandon, Leslie, and I headed to lunch.

"I can't wait for Swirl!" Leslie said in a singsong voice when I told her about my letter.

"Me either," I said, my voice dripping with sarcasm. "Obviously."

Brandon put an arm around my shoulders. "You know you could always go with me, baby."

"In your dreams, hun."

CHAPTER THREE

Dear Anika,

Of course this Rhett guy (is that even a real name?) would ask you out. You're a very attractive girl. Hell, I probably would have asked you if I was in high school with you! Lord knows I could use some fun. Over here, the most fun we have is playing games of frisbee or soccer, or maybe watching a movie from time to time. Usually, it's just going through the motions of work, but some things really shake me up. There was a suicide bomber yesterday as we were driving through a town, and one guy I was starting to get close to was killed. It made everything seem so short, like it could all be over tomorrow... What do you think happens when you die, Anika?

Yours,
Shawn

PS: Would you to go Swirl with me if I was there? :)

. . .

Dear Shawn,

I would love to go to swirl with you, but I wouldn't want to deprive America of your services! As to what I think about death... I honestly don't know. I was raised a (very strict) Southern Baptist by my parents, but I'm still confused. According to my religion, there's a lot of fire and brimstone and it's all a little hard to swallow. I do think God is real, and if he's everywhere, there's no point in me going to church to know Him.

The thing is, I think you can see God in every situation—sometimes you can just tell. Like when someone picks up books for someone else, or you see an old couple holding hands... Everyone has good and bad.

I guess what I'm saying is I don't know how someone could draw the line to where you go when you die... I don't know. But if anyone goes to Heaven, I definitely think it would be the guys risking their lives for everyone else.

Always,
Anika

CHAPTER FOUR

"ANIKA, are you really not going with anyone?" Brandon asked me after basketball practice.

He always gave me rides home because he was about the closest thing I had to a neighbor—even though we lived two miles away from each other—and because the only vehicle I had to my name was an old beater pickup that probably couldn't make it to town and back.

"Other than third-wheeling with Leslie and Skye?" I asked.

I ended up texting one of my girlfriends from McClellan to see if she would go to Swirl with me since Leslie had a date. McClellan was a bigger town about half an hour away, and we played them in sports sometimes. Since Roderdale didn't have a movie theatre or a grocery store, everyone usually went to McClellan for shopping or entertainment. I figured between Skye, Leslie, and Bran, I didn't really need a date.

"Is there something you should be telling me?" He raised an eyebrow.

"About?"

"So, let's say that I like women, so I'm oriented north, and you like—"

"Okay, okay! I like guys," I said to stop any more of his metaphors.

He laughed and then went on. "Well, if that's so, there's a guy from here you should consider."

"Who?"

"Well—"

"And if it's Rhett, I'm going to scream."

"No!" He laughed again. "It's Kyle."

"Kyle likes me?"

"Maybe, but don't go getting all full of yourself."

"Kyle *Rayford* likes me?"

Brandon nodded. "I thought you were supposed to be the smart one."

Kyle Rayford. I never thought he would be even remotely interested in me. We were both seniors and in the same class, but he and Melissa had been in an on-again, off-again relationship since sophomore year. Rumors had it that this breakup was final, but rumors around Roderdale usually didn't turn out to be true. Melissa was arguably the prettiest girl in Roderdale, and it would take a lot to make Kyle stay away from her.

It only fit that Kyle would be her boyfriend; if Melissa was the prettiest girl in Roderdale, Kyle was the best-looking guy I'd ever seen. He wasn't extremely tall or short at 5'11" and he was built strong from growing up on a ranch.

His family farmed about ten miles down the road from my family. On the few occasions we'd worked together over the past summer and I'd seen him with his shirt off, I'd had to forcibly peel my eyes off his abs. His cheeks were permanently blushed, which set off the prettiest brown eyes I had ever seen on a guy. The rest of his skin was flawless. Most of my girlfriends from other schools were quick to ask if I could get them an in with him, and I'd always had to say no.

"Kyle Rayford?" I repeated.

"Kyle Rayford," Bran mimicked. "Interested?"

Why couldn't Kyle have asked me out freshman year? Before I'd "dated" Chris and before Kyle'd started dating Melissa.

"It's kinda last-minute," I hedged.

"Yeah, but Lisa and I are going," he told me.

"Lisa?"

I hadn't known Bran to date a lot of girls. One of the main reasons we could be friends was we never had boyfriends or girlfriends that got jealous of our friendship... but now he was going to Swirl with a freshman?

"Yeah."

I sighed loudly. If Brandon had a date, we wouldn't be guaranteed to have guys to dance with.

"Fine, I'll go with Kyle. *As friends*!"

"Well, text him later or tell him at school tomorrow, I guess," Bran said.

We talked about school until we pulled up to my house. I didn't ask him about Lisa, and he didn't needle me about Kyle. I guessed that's what I liked about my friendship with Bran; we understood each other.

CHAPTER FIVE

"ANIKA!" Mom yelled down the stairs to where Leslie and I were getting ready.

"What?" I shot a pained look at Leslie and Skye.

Skye smiled sympathetically. Mom was one of those parents who was always hardest on the oldest, which meant she frequently used lines like "you're older, you should know better" or "you're setting a lousy example." She also thought I needed a job on top of what I already did—basketball at the moment, helping on the ranch, and a 3.6 GPA. I wasn't Supergirl, but that didn't stop her.

"Brandon's here!" Mom called.

"Can you send him down?"

She didn't say anything for a few minutes, and then I heard Brandon plod down the stairs. He was wearing black pinstriped pants with a black shirt and a hot pink tie.

"Well, hello, James Bond," I teased him.

"Just thought I'd drop by to check how I look," he told us while he looked in my mirror and tried to tame the cowlick at the back of his head.

"Skye's great at hair," I said.

Brandon flopped his arms to his side. "Why didn't you say so earlier?"

I shrugged.

"Help!" he said to Skye.

She grabbed a bottle of hairspray, and in a matter of seconds, had flattened the pesky hairs.

"Perfect!" I said.

Leslie, Skye, and I were all done with our hair and makeup, so we went to my room and put on our dresses. Leslie had a high-waisted, bright red, sparkly dress that fell about three inches above her knees. Skye wore a strapless orange dress that showed off her muscled shoulders. I felt more than a little self-conscious standing next to them.

"You look so pretty," Skye said.

Skye was quiet, but she was one of the most honest people I knew—and not in a blurt-the-first-thing-that-comes-to-mind way like Leslie was—so I felt a little better.

I glanced at the clock. "Bran, you better go get Lisa."

He promptly left, and we waited for our dates. Leslie's date showed up first, and, of course, they had to take a few pictures before leaving. Kyle arrived shortly after they left, and when I saw him, it was hard to pick my jaw up off the floor.

His dirty blond hair was still a bit damp from the shower, which created a perfectly messy look. He was wearing khaki pants and a light blue shirt with the sleeves rolled up. He stood a few inches taller than me, even when I was wearing heels.

"You look great, Anika," he said with a warm smile. He had one of those smiles that sent weaker girls—okay, and me—swooning.

"Thanks." I grinned at him. "You too."

"Let me get a picture real quick before you leave," Mom

ordered. Dad stood beside her while Kyle put his arm around my waist, and posed for the photo.

"Okay, you and Skye now!" Mom said.

Kyle dropped his arm from my waist and went to stand by Dad.

"How's your old man doing?" Dad asked Kyle.

Kyle's dad and my dad were really good friends, and we used to all hang out together when we were younger, but after Kyle started dating Melissa, that stopped. Kyle spent his weekends with her, and I didn't feel like being a third wheel with two old men.

"He's good," Kyle said. "Been busy putting up a new fence."

"Okay, let's go!" I said after Mom had taken at least a dozen pictures.

Kyle drove Skye and me into town, and having Skye there helped take the pressure off. Bran had said Kyle was interested in me, and I didn't want to send him the wrong message when I still wasn't sure how I felt.

When we got to the gym, I found someone to dance with Skye, and Kyle took my hand and led me to the dance-floor aka gym floor.

Kyle had a lot of things going for him, but dancing was not one of them. We stumbled through the slow dance, and we eventually decided that I should keep my toes on top of his feet so he wouldn't step on me.

Toe injuries aside, he was the best dance partner I'd ever had.

Kyle wasn't any better at the fast dances, but we had fun in our little group doing Kyle impressions. I was just glad that his lack of skill had taken the attention away from my own horrible moves.

We didn't dance all of the slow songs together so we

were able to dance with our other friends from school. Even though we weren't dating, I was pleased when Leslie pointed out that Kyle had refused to dance with Melissa. I only got to dance with Bran once because—as I anticipated—he spent most of the night hand-in-hand with Lisa.

The last song played too soon.

Kyle walked up to me and stuck his hand out.

I lifted my hand to put it in his.

"Wait," he said.

"What?" *Now* he decided he didn't want to dance with me again?

"Would you be willing to sign a waiver for your feet?"

CHAPTER SIX

Dear Anika,

I know what you mean about seeing God in people. After the bombing, I watched a soldier cradle a little kid for hours because her parents had both died in the blast. Neither spoke the same language, but there was something between them. Maybe it was kind of like what you were talking about, just God between them.

It's so different from Texas here. Back home, if someone was having trouble, people would all work together and help them out. Here, one person could be starving to death, the next could be plump as a pumpkin, and neither cares. They've all got their own problems going on, so they don't even acknowledge each other.

I thought coming here I'd feel like I was making a difference, but not everyone seems to think so. One person might think I'm the kindest hero in the world and another thinks we're destroying their country. You never know what's going to happen. One day you could be playing Frisbee with the guys or skyping your mom, and the next it could be over. But I can't believe life stops just like that.

Yours,
Shawn

Dear Shawn,

I can't even imagine what that would be like. Just know people here think you're a hero.

So how have you been? Life's been pretty much the same for me... School, homework, sports, chores, sleep, repeat... except for Swirl. I ended up getting a date! A guy named Kyle asked me—well, he kind of asked Bran and Bran asked me—and I told him we could go as friends. I don't know if I'm ready to start dating again, and I'm definitely not sure about committing to anything so close to graduation, but maybe that's a story for another day...

My best friend Brandon surprised me by going with a FRESHMAN! Don't you think that's pretty bad? I mean a senior and a freshman going together? I know it's Brandon, and he was really sweet to her, but still. I'm glad my little brother won't be in high school 'til next year when I've graduated. His future girlfriend should be glad, too. I probably won't be the most accommodating big sister, but that's me. :)

Always,
Anika

***

"HEY, Anika, do you want to come sit with me and some of the guys today?" Kyle asked as we walked to lunch.

His invitation really surprised me. I had told him we were just going to Swirl as friends, and we'd had a great time together, mainly because it was a pretty carefree environment. Except for the fact that his ex-girlfriend, who also happens to be point guard on our basketball team, was giving me the death glare all morning. I was a little nervous to see how she'd act with me in practice that evening.

"I was going to sit with Leslie today," I said. To be honest, I sat with her every day.

He smiled. "She can come, too, if she wants."

Two girls sitting at an all-guy table? The world makes sense again. Not.

"Oh, sounds good," I said, trying to play it cool. "I'm sure she won't mind."

I wasn't sure why I was so nervous. Kyle and I were just friends, and I didn't have intentions of starting a relationship. He hadn't made any comments about dating or liking me or anything at the dance, although, he had told me how beautiful he thought I was during the last slow dance...

We walked into the cafeteria together, and I quickly found Leslie and told her what was going on. She squealed loud enough for Kyle to hear us, and my cheeks blushed bright red as Kyle tried not to laugh.

"Leslie!" I whispered. "Shut up! Are you going to sit with us?"

"Yes! Are you guys going out?!"

"No, we're just eating lunch at the same table."

"Suuuuure," she said, then picked up her tray to join us.

"Sorry," I said to Kyle under my breath when Leslie wasn't looking. "She has high hopes for you and me."

"Hey, so do I."

CHAPTER SEVEN

Dear Anika,

Why do you have a problem with Brandon dating Lisa? Do you not like age differences? It sounds like Brandon's a pretty solid guy, and you should trust him to pick who he wants to date. I know it's hard sometimes.

When my friend here went on his first date in high school, I was so confused! She was the most awkward girl he could have possibly found at our school, but it worked out perfectly. She was really smart, and they both had someone on their level. They've been married for two years now, and he has a baby on the way. So just trust Brandon, and see how it goes. It may not even last a week.

As for your little brother, he's a lucky kid! It's always nice to have someone to look out for you and help you make choices. But please don't come with a shotgun when she meets the family! Leave it to your dad! He's done pretty good with you.

Yours,
Shawn

Dear Shawn,

Yes, I have a problem with that age difference. I've dated two boys in my life. It went well with my first boyfriend, but something just didn't click, you know? Like when we kissed I didn't feel a spark or anything. But when I broke up with him, he cried, and it was really hard.

I was still a freshman when my next boyfriend and I started dating. It was bad. He was a senior, and he convinced me that if we had sex, we would be closer, and our relationship could survive while he went to college. He said he wanted to marry me when I graduated. I didn't get pregnant or anything, but he broke up with me the next day—in a text. "You're a great friend, but I can't think of you as a girlfriend anymore," were his exact words.

I don't think anyone except Brandon knows about it. I didn't even tell Leslie because she's not very good at keeping secrets. If anyone knew, they wouldn't see me the same way. I was supposed to be setting an example for my siblings, and look what I did. I disappointed myself. I can't trust myself to get serious with a boy. I wasn't ready, but now I know how experienced seniors are with freshmen girls. They know what girls want to hear, and they will do anything to get a girl to do what they want—even break her heart. I know it's not fair for me to judge everyone that way, but I'm flawed, and I've definitely proved it. Next time I get close to a guy, nothing is happening until I'm MARRIED. Well, except kissing.

Always,
Anika

I SIGHED as I put the finished letter into a starch white envelope. Part of me was terrified to tell him this stuff about myself, but part of me felt totally safe telling him. If I was honest with myself, I was more nervous to tell him about my promise to abstain from sex until marriage than my stupid mistake with Chris.

Shawn and I had never met, never even seen each other aside from a wallet-sized picture, but I liked him, and I supposed that distance gave me the courage to tell him everything. It felt freeing to share my secret with someone other than Brandon, but I doubted Shawn would want to write me again after he learned about me. Either he'd think I was a prude, or he'd think I was loose. Girls had sex every day, but I expected more of myself, and I was sure Shawn did, too.

CHAPTER EIGHT

Dear Anika,

I am so sorry. I had no idea. I think you might be wrong about how people see you. (I definitely know what a small town is like, though, so that bit may not work in your favor.) People probably think of you as an independent, strong, cautious girl who had her heart broken. I feel your pain. Shortly after I left to serve overseas, the girl I had been dating for about a year decided she liked someone else more, but I think she liked him more while we were still dating... if you know what I mean. I'm not going to lie and say I'm over it, and I'm definitely not as strong as you, but I'm slowly moving on.

They say time heals all wounds, and that may be true, but you can still see the scar that reminds you of the pain that caused it. I'm hoping that I can find a girl to help me forget the scar. Make the pain worth it somehow. That has yet to happen, though. In the meantime, you and I will stick together, right? Friends make the world a better place. Just stay happy (like I know you're doing), and someone will find you and be so afraid to lose you he'll never be a dick. I hope.

Yours,
Shawn

Dear Shawn,

Thank you so much. You described it so well. You're right about friends making the world a better place, and I know you're making the world a better place wherever you are. Do you think when you get home your ex will want you again? Maybe she was just afraid to lose you and found another guy to hide the scar before it had a chance to fade? She shouldn't have done it, but when you love someone, you build walls to see if they want to climb them or knock them down to get to you. Life can be a test sometimes, and some people just test better than others. So far, I think I suck at testing!

When are you coming back? I had a great idea that we can hang out and you can take me shopping, so I can get the military discount!! Ha ha. Just kidding. But really, it would be nice to meet you so I can talk to you in person.

Always,
Anika

I'D STARTED LOOKING FORWARD to Shawn's letters more and more and always asked Miss B. at the beginning of English if he had sent any more. The only people I talked to about Shawn were Leslie, Bran, and I'd told Skye about him after homecoming.

Shawn and I were starting to get close, and I worried I might be tiptoeing some sort of fine line. If people started to make this more than it was, they might cancel the pen pal program altogether, and I had enough to worry about without losing contact with a soldier overseas.

After I carefully sealed and addressed the envelope, I felt a tap on my shoulder from behind. Miss B. just left the room to make copies, so the class had relaxed. A low murmur filled the room, but Bran still whispered when he handed me a note. "From Kyle."

I glanced at Kyle, and he smiled widely, eliciting another death glare from Melissa. He seemed oblivious, though.

Wanna go to a movie in McClellan later tonight? It's on me.
K

I flipped the paper over and wrote my reply, then handed it to Brandon, who passed it to Kyle.

I got the popcorn :)
A

CHAPTER NINE

I SHOWERED in the locker room after practice so Kyle and I could just leave from the school. Then, I called Mom and let her know what was going on. Luckily, she'd been getting progressively more lenient throughout my senior year.

In about half an hour, Kyle met me by the front of the school in his Chevy. Maybe it was just me, but seeing a boy in a truck was a turn-on.

"Hey," I said as I got in and put my backpack and gym bag in the backseat.

He put the pickup in gear. "How was practice?"

Kyle had a wide smile on his face that made me feel at ease.

"Oh, okay, I guess. Yours?"

"Coach made us run because the sophomore boys got detention."

"That sucks," I sympathized.

"Pretty much." Kyle glanced over at me and did a double take. Then he reached out and caught a strand of my hair between his fingers.

"I never noticed your hair was curly."

The beginnings of a blush warmed my cheeks. "Maybe you were too busy with Melissa," I teased.

A dark expression marred his face. "Anika, that's over."

"I know." I didn't like where this conversation was going.

"And you're single."

It wasn't fair. Kyle was driving, so he didn't have to look at me while he was talking.

"Yeah, but—" I began, but he quickly interrupted me.

"Are you still hung up over Chris?"

A part of me I tried to keep in a locked emotional drawer opened up. The huge rock of pain sunk in my chest, and I remembered seeing Chris for the last time before he left for college. We'd run into each other at the Walmart in McClellan; he had been doing some last-minute shopping before leaving.

His eyes didn't have the loving look I remembered from the times we had spent together. The ripping sensation I felt when he'd dumped me tore through my chest.

"No," I lied.

"Anika," he said, taking his eyes off the road to look at me. "I know what happened."

Oh God. "That was a long time ago, and—"

"Chris was an asshole. You can't blame yourself for what happened. Other girls fell for it, too. Melissa did."

"Wait, what?" I thought I was the only girl Chris had dated his senior year.

"Right after he broke up with you, he went to Melissa and acted all hurt, like you had dumped him. He told her how she could comfort him, and she did. And when he left her, she came to me. She was a mess. It took her so long to move past it and open up."

"That's how you guys started going out? Because of me?"

"Anika! Come on!" he said, but I could tell there was a hint of a smile in his voice. "Chris was good at the game. Melissa and I... Well, that's another story."

"And are you saying you're over her?"

He stared at the road. "Our relationship was so far gone I couldn't do anything with her except break up. I don't even think she misses me," he confided. "I think she just misses the status."

My heart went out to him. It was easy to see how dating someone like Kyle could be more of an ego trip than anything.

When I was dating Chris, I'd thought I was so cool. I had the 6'2" senior quarterback with *me* at prom. It was *me* he held tight and kissed. It was *me* he wanted to hang out with, not any of the other girls—or so I'd thought. Maybe Melissa's ego was hurting more than her heart.

"I'm sorry."

"Don't be. We have a few months until college, and until then, I want as many friends as possible."

He smiled warmly at me, and I couldn't help but feel disappointed. Two great guys had said they wanted to be friends with me. Was it my fault they didn't want any more than that?

CHAPTER TEN

Dear Anika,

I'm pretty sure giving you my military discount wouldn't work out too well toward the code of ethics we're supposed to follow! But maybe it can be a gift! About my ex...it's over. She's engaged to that guy. I actually just got a letter from her telling me I'm invited to the wedding, and I should be home in time to make it. Too bad I burned the invite.

Yours,
Shawn

Dear Shawn,

I don't blame you one bit! Yesterday, Kyle and I went to a movie together as friends and he told me a lot about my ex—and his, I guess—that I didn't even know. I found out that Chris slept with another girl in my class—who also happens to be Kyle's ex—before he left for college. He definitely left memories in this town, and I can't really say they're good. I may be hurt, but I never thought Melissa probably feels the same way. I guess it's good to realize you're not the only person with a broken heart.

Well, it's not really broken, I guess there's just a scar there, like what you told me a while back. It'll fade eventually. So tell me how everything is there. Saved any lives? When are you coming home?

Always,
Anika

***

"HEY, HOW'D THE DATE GO?" Leslie was one of many girls to ask me this on Monday. I hadn't told anyone except for Bran and Leslie, and Kyle didn't seem like the kind of guy who would blab to everyone, but, like always, word got out.

We were between classes, and the hallway was about as crowded as it could get in such a small school. I looked around to make sure no one was listening in.

I sighed and said the four words I had told everyone else who'd asked: "It wasn't a date."

"You didn't kiss?" she probed.

"Nope."

"Hold hands?"

"Nope."

"Hug?!" she was starting to get worried.

I laughed. "Yes, we hugged. It was like hugging Bran."

"A tall, sexy Bran!"

"What's this about tall and sexy?" Kyle's low voice hummed behind us.

Leslie turned bright pink and opened her mouth as if to make up an excuse. Nothing came out.

After watching Leslie suffer for a moment, I answered him. "Oh, we were just talking about our 'date.'"

"Oh," he winked at me. "The part after was super sexy, huh?"

"Kyle!" I whined at the sight of Leslie's face lighting up.

He laughed. "See you at lunch, An."

"See ya." I watched as he went into the classroom.

"'The part after was really sexy,'" Leslie quoted. "Really sexy?!"

"Tell you later!"

CHAPTER ELEVEN

Dear Anika,

It's alright to admit that you're hurt. It's sad to say it, but that's how you know it happened. I know there are some things you really wished NEVER happened, but one day, you'll look back, and it'll be alright. Think about how many days you've lived compared to the ones you remember. It's a scary number, isn't it? Do you want to look back and only remember the negative? Yes, this Chris guy was an asshole, but you did feel loved for a while, didn't you? That's one of the best feelings in the world. You also have a learning experience to carry on with you.

There's probably also friends you wouldn't have made otherwise, and just different things you were able to do BECAUSE you had a boyfriend his age. It was awful, what he did, but you wouldn't be the amazing Anika I know today if it wasn't for him, so for that, I'm thankful.

Now you asked me a question, so I guess I have to answer it!

Today, we were driving to another base, and one of the hummers ahead of me ran over a land mine. At first, I didn't know what was happening, and then I saw chunks of metal flying through the air. We lost four soldiers. For that split second, when a bomb goes off or you hear gunfire, it's you against the world to see who's the bigger man. I haven't lost yet, but you never know. Have you ever felt that way?

Yours,
Shawn

Dear Shawn,

I guess you're right, but I don't know about me being amazing. I have felt like it's just me against the world, but it definitely wasn't in the literal sense like you are using. If something like that happened to me, I'd just want to curl up in a little ball, hide somewhere, and never come out. I can't believe how brave you all are to just keep going after something like that...

I love the feeling in Volleyball when I take a ball back to the serving line. I bounce it once, twice, three times, and then I throw it up in the air. Most people hate serving, but to me, it's my favorite part. The game starts with a serve. Back there, on the line, you have the opportunity to decide how the game goes. If the ball hits the net, you lose a valuable point. If you make it go over, you get to choose the weakest opponent and make it go to them. It's all about strategy. But for a second, after the ball leaves your hands, you're in limbo. It could go over, under, into, but either way, it's all on you. It's lame, I know. It's just a game, but I love it. Oh, and Shawn, you forgot to tell me when you're coming back.

Always,
Anika

***

"TIME TO SPILL." Leslie was giving me a ride home tonight, specifically, so she could ask me all the questions she wanted.

I leaned against the headrest in her car. Leslie drove a cute, little red Prius, and she wasn't afraid to take advantage of its speed.

I thought back to the conversation and mentally cursed Kyle for making it seem like a bigger deal to Leslie than it really was. He knew I would get the fifth degree later on. After a few years of not hanging out with him anymore, I'd forgotten how mischievous he could be. That so-called "seductive" twinkle in his "luscious" blue eyes... not seductive at all. It was actually a playful spark!

"There really wasn't anything sexy about it," I said truthfully.

She glared at me for a little bit longer than she should have and had to jerk the car back into the right lane.

"Les!" I cried. "Eyes on the road!"

"Then dish!"

"Okay, we hugged after he dropped me off back at my house, and when I was about to go, he pulled me back into another hug. I had my chin kinda rested on his chest, and we just looked into each other's eyes for a little bit. It was really sweet. And then he told me goodnight, and that was it."

"You *hugged* Kyle Rayford! You had a moment with Kyle freakin' Rayford!"

"I guess I did," I said with a little smile.

CHAPTER TWELVE

Dear Anika,

Sports are really easy to compare to war, but in war, the stakes are higher. You're playing for your life, not for a state championship. I can't even describe the feeling.

I'm not telling you when I'm coming back. All I'm saying is, one day, you'll go to school, and you'll see me in class.

Yours,
Shawn

Dear Shawn,

In what world is that fair? You get to come to class without me even knowing when!?!? Shawn! Tell me! Does that mean you're off soon? When are you going back over? How many more years do you have in service? How long are you going to be here? I need to know! I do NOT handle surprises well AT

ALL. So, you better tell me now before I go crazy!! K? K. Thanks.

Always,
Anika

"HE'S COMING TO SEE YOU?" Leslie practically screamed, attracting attention from Brandon and Kyle, who were sitting with us at lunch.

Kyle swallowed his food. "Who's coming to see you?"

"Jus—" I began, but Leslie cut me off.

"Just the sexy solider pen pal she got assigned to in English class! I don't know how she got so lucky, but he has a friend, right? Maybe I'll have some eye candy that day, too! Yay!" Then—get this—she actually squealed like the dramatic girls in movies do.

Brandon cringed. "Leslie! I want to be able to hear when I get older."

Leslie ignored him. "Wait, does he have tattoos? Please tell me he has tattoos."

Brandon made a crack about what Leslie could get tattooed, which led to a lot of bickering. I was thankful when the bell rang and we all rose to scrape our plates.

"Want to go ride horses after practice?" Kyle whispered in my ear.

Kyle wasn't the stereotypical country boy. He wore fitted, stylish jeans, and almost always brand name shirts that hugged his body. Country was a side of Kyle not a lot of people got to see, but I had just because our dads had been really close friends pretty much forever.

"It'll be dark and cold by the time we get started," I pointed out.

He shrugged. "We'll go bareback, and night riding is the best."

He smiled and didn't wait for an answer. "I'll pick you up after practice."

CHAPTER THIRTEEN

"SO WHY ARE WE DOING THIS?" It was cold and dark outside, just like I'd said it would be. Several stars dotted the inky, black sky, casting an eerie glow over the Rayfords' barn.

His smile practically illuminated the stables. "Because it's fun."

I shook my head and took one of the bridles from him. I walked up to one of his horses—a tan and white paint—and put the bridle on. After I was finished, I led her out of the stall and handed the reins to Kyle.

"Wanna leg up?" he asked.

I nodded and he helped me onto the horse. Its warm skin against me and Kyle's thick coat—that he'd generously offered—protected me from the biting spring air. He handed the reins up to me, his hand lingering on mine just long enough to send chills that definitely weren't from the wind up my spine.

A smile still laced his full lips as he turned and jumped onto his horse. I was so surprised that his grace from the basketball court translated to riding.

"Nice," I commented.

"Thanks."

"So, I have a question," he told me. The moonlight glinted off his skin and hair, making it look more silver than blond.

"Okay, shoot."

He leaned forward on his horse and stroked its neck. "What would you do if you had to choose between being with someone who wants you or being alone because you can't have the person you want?"

"Is this about you?"

He laid against the horse's neck. "Maybe."

"Why can't you have her?" I asked confusedly. Kyle could have any girl he wanted.

He laughed. "Don't over analyze it, An. Just answer it."

"Okay, okay!" I laughed, too. Just hearing his laugh it could put anyone in a better mood. "I think it's scary to be alone, but if this is the person you really, really love, it wouldn't be so terrible. It would help if you guys could be friends and maybe, one day, have it evolve into something else. But if you decided to be with the person who wanted you, you could be cheating the person who wants the girl who wants you. You know what I'm saying?"

"I think so," he said.

"Now I'm really curious," I told him. "Who's this girl?"

"It's you."

"It's—wait... what?"

I had to admit that we'd been getting a lot closer, but I never thought in a million years he'd actually want to seriously date me. I just thought it was great that I got to hang out with a really cool, nice guy besides Bran. I'd be lying if I said I'd never imagined what it would be like to be Kyle's girlfriend. He was a good boyfriend to Melissa—handsome, kind. Kyle Rayford wanted me? No way.

"Let me ask you another question," he said. "Have you ever thought about you and me... as a couple?"

Honestly? "Well, not really," I lied.

"Why not?" he wondered.

"I guess I never thought someone like you would want someone like me when you could have someone like Melissa."

"Please," he said. "Quit playing that self-deprecating act."

That stung. "It's not an act!"

He sat up. "Ever since that whole deal with Chris, you haven't dated anyone. Not one single guy."

"So?"

"So? So stop blowing off every guy who even gets close!"

"I didn't come out here to get a lecture on dating from a guy who couldn't stay with his girlfriend for more than two months in a row."

His eyes got wide, and I could tell he was hurt, even in the darkness. He reined his horse so it turned toward the barn.

"Kyle, I—"

"Let's go back," he said.

He kicked his horse and galloped away. I dug my heels into the sides of my horse and wrapped my legs tight around its belly so its lope wouldn't throw me off. But, at that point, I probably deserved it.

CHAPTER FOURTEEN

Dear Anika,

Why do you want to know so badly? Some of the best things in life are the things you weren't expecting. Maybe when I come, you won't be prepared, so when I talk to you, you can say what's truly in your heart and on your mind, not what you've had time to think about and prepare for that specific day. I'm coming soon, though. I WILL tell you that I am still overseas, and I'm looking forward to meeting the girl who's blown me away with words. See you soon, Anika.

Yours,
Shawn

I SIGHED when I read the letter and tucked it into my backpack. English was one of my favorite classes now. Every day, when we arrived, Miss B. had a handful of letters she would give to the lucky people whose soldier had written back. Every day, I looked for Shawn to be in the class and was disappointed when he didn't pop out from behind the door and say, "Hello, Anika. Nice to meet you."

I imagined a wide grin making his eyes sparkle like they had in the picture. I could practically see the slight dimples adding to his boyish, yet somehow strong features. I wondered what it would feel like to have his arms around me—hardened from months of labor and training in the military. How his full—*stop*! Shawn was just a friend. I'd never even seen him in person! I tried to shake thoughts of him and me and our imaginary romantic relationship. Clearly, I was no good at love.

Kyle hadn't said a word to me since he dropped me off at my house the night before, and I didn't expect him to break the silence anytime soon. I'd tried to talk to him and apologize on the way home, but he had kept his mouth shut.

Maybe that was good because I couldn't say anything else to mess it up more. I didn't even know how I felt about it. I wasn't sure where I was going to college yet, but everyone always told me I shouldn't tie myself down until then—that I would meet a lot of guys—but would any of them even compare to Kyle?

Dear Shawn,

I'm glad that I've blown you away. I have to admit I'm really nervous for you to come. What if you meet me and you realize that I'm not all you expected me to be? What if you come and see someone else who's totally gorgeous, like my best friend Leslie, and don't want to write me anymore? Every day, a whole new load of "what if's" enter my mind, and I am even more stressed about meeting you. What if it would be better to keep writing letters? What if I never see you again? What if you never want to see me again?

Always,
Anika

CHAPTER FIFTEEN

"ARE you ready for basketball to be over?" Bran asked. "'Cause I sure as hell am."

We were on our way home after what had turned out to be an especially hard practice for the boys. Both teams were tense with Substate just around the corner. It was the first time in over ten years that Roderdale had both a girls' and boys' team to qualify for Substate, and both teams were desperate to make it to State.

"It's better than track," I reminded him.

"Our coach is an ass," he reminded me.

I nodded, and we rode in silence the rest of the way to my house. Bran probably was too tired to ask me about Kyle, and I was too confused to try and make sense of it with him.

"See you tomorrow," he told me as I got out of his vehicle.

"See ya."

I dropped my pencil the second I heard my phone vibrate, glad to have an excuse to stop working on homework. I looked at the screen as my phone danced a little circle around where it sat on my desk. One new text message. Of course.

I was so sick of texting! I missed eighth grade when it was cool to talk on the phone and no one had unlimited texting... No one wanted to have an actual conversation anymore; they would rather talk with smiley faces and emojis. It was all a waste of time.

Kyle R: Hey, is it too late to call?

Thank God for people like Kyle. For a second, I forgot that we hadn't talked since we'd ridden horses and I'd made that snappy comment about him and Melissa. Was he going to break up with me? I knew we weren't dating, but it might be just as hard to lose him as a friend.

I texted him to tell him he could call, and within minutes, my phone was vibrating again.

"Hey Anika," he said before I even got a chance to say hello.

"What's up?"

My stomach was tying itself in knots.

"Just wanted to talk. Think I could sneak into your house?"

I let out a nervous laugh that sounded more like a snort. When we were in eighth grade, he got an award for good citizenship. Kyle was the last person I expected to go sneaking around, but when he didn't laugh with me, I realized he was serious.

"Maybe... talk on the trampoline out in our tree row?" I suggested.

Mom had decided the tree row was a convenient place to put our trampoline. Nestled between the spacey rows of evergreen trees, no one could see the "eyesore."

"I'll call you when I get close," he said.

"Okay."

I slipped on a pair of sweatpants and a thick jacket. It might have been optimistic of me, but I grabbed the comforter off my bed so we wouldn't be cold while we talked outside.

I was hoping he had the sense not to drive all the way up in our driveway, and was relieved when I got a call fifteen minutes later saying he was in our tree row, waiting for me.

"Do you need help getting down from your room?" he asked, ever the gentleman.

"No. My parents sleep downstairs. Dad thinks it's too hot upstairs."

Soon, I was outside with Kyle, lying under a thick blanket on the trampoline and staring at the sky. It was cloudy, but the moon penetrated the cloud cover to cast a silver blue light over us.

He said only a few words of greeting, and we were lying side-by-side, our weight rolling us closer to each other on the trampoline. I was forced to decide between suffering the spring chill or falling into his warm body.

"I'm sorry for freaking out," he finally said.

I was gazing above, mostly to avoid the look of disappointment I was sure was on his face, but at those words, I turned to face him. The icy fear in my heart melted ever so slightly.

"It's okay," I told him, because I didn't know what else to say.

"It's just... I don't know how a girl like you... I mean you're athletic, you're good in school, you're so sweet, and you're one of the most beautiful girls in the conference. You have plenty of options, and I don't understand why you shove them all away."

Tears stung my eyes and started to multiply. I felt so pathetic for crying because someone was being nice to me.

"It's just I thought since Chris—"

"Stop," he interrupted me. "Do you want me to tell you how guys work?"

I replied in a small voice. "Please."

"Okay, guys are in it for one of three things: to show up their friends, to get laid, or because they actually like and respect a girl and want to make her happy." The rusty springs of the trampoline creaked as he shifted his weight and rested his head on his hand. "Because they see her inner beauty that just shines through. They can see that her eyes light up when she's talking about her friends or her siblings... That she can be rough-and-tumble on the ranch or tender with a child. They want her to look like that when she's talking about them. They think maybe they'd like to see that girl grow old because that spark will always be there."

He stroked my cheek with his thumb.

"So, which are you?" I asked.

"Oh, I'm in it for the physical, of course." His eyes were dancing in the silver light.

I lifted my arm and shoved him on his shoulder.

"What do you think?" he asked.

"The last one?"

He nodded, and a small smile played over his face.

"Now the real question is, do you want me, too?"

I hesitated, the time Chris asked me out in the forefront of my mind. It was toward the end of my freshman year, and Leslie had gotten us invited to a party with some of the seniors. I'd felt so cool with a beer in my hand, leaning against a pickup by a shop out in the country. Chris had walked right up to me and put his arm around my shoulders. He was so tall, and I'd felt so warm nestled in under his arm.

We'd been standing in a group of people, but he'd leaned down and whispered in my ear, the sweet smell of alcohol on his breath.

"You are so beautiful."

I was so dumbfounded that the only thing I could say was, "What?"

We'd talked some throughout the year—just about as much as was normal for a senior and a freshman, but he'd never really hinted at being interested in me.

"You're gorgeous," he'd said. "Those blue eyes."

His face had been so close to mine that his breath tickled my skin and raised goose bumps on my neck.

"Go out with me," he'd said.

It hadn't been a question. Of course I would go out with him. He was athletic, attractive, funny, and he was a senior. Not a lot of freshman girls ever got asked out by seniors, let alone seniors as good-looking as Chris.

My mind snapped back to the present when I heard Kyle sigh.

"You're thinking about him, aren't you?"

"Yeah," I admitted. "I am."

"Do you miss him?"

"No," I answered truthfully. I didn't know if I'd ever really missed him. It was like I'd built up how much I liked him in my mind so I wouldn't feel so horrible for giving him my virginity.

I rolled to my stomach and lifted myself onto my elbows so I could more easily see Kyle's face. His shaggy hair fell in a perfect mess across his forehead. Judging by the way he knit his eyebrows together, he was deep in thought.

"What is it then?" His voice was so tender, genuinely curious.

"My trust," I answered. "It sucks. I believed all of Chris's lies. Then there's a guy who deserves my trust... and I just can't find a way to give it to him."

The whisper of the wind in the trees and our steady breathing filled the silence. Suddenly nervous about what Kyle thought about what I'd said, I kept my mouth shut and let my eyes wonder around our tree row. A lone jack rabbit darted between two low branches.

"Kyle?"

"Yeah?"

"I'm sorry." I sighed heavily.

He knew what I was saying; I was too afraid. The pain was apparent in his eyes, and I never wanted to cause that.

"Don't be." He laid on his back.

It took a second for me to build up the courage to ask my next question.

"Do you ever miss Melissa?"

"I was talking to my youth pastor about that right before Swirl. I was thinking about how I missed having someone to hold and talk to at night. I almost asked her to Swirl instead of you. You know, to try and make up. And I told him, 'I know it's not God's will for us to be together, but it is His will for me to be happy, right?'" Kyle's lips twisted into a sad smile. "He was really understanding about it. He told me I'd care about Melissa for the rest of my life. I mean, she was my first love. But he also told me I'd meet someone who mattered more."

His lips trembled for a second.

"And then there wouldn't be any room in my heart to love these two girls the same way."

Until I met someone who mattered more. Was it Shawn

helping me move on from Chris? Or was it Kyle? Or was it time? I knew I was still hurting from Chris, and I was pretty sure that part of me would hurt until the day I died, but I had been getting better... stronger.

"And you found that someone?" I asked.

He nodded. "I think so."

Kyle opened his arms and pulled me into a tight hug that cradled me across his warm chest. I felt the steady rhythm of his heart, and I felt mine break in two. Shawn was still in my life, and though he may not have known it, he had become more than a pen pal to me. Kyle was the best guy anyone could ask for. I let the moment wash away the confusion and listened to the sweet melody of the wind, his heart, and our breaths.

CHAPTER SIXTEEN

I HAD terrifying dreams after Kyle left and I finally fell into bed. My nightmares took me back to that night... the night when I lost my virginity. Something was wrong, as always. Maybe it was the way Chris didn't look at me lovingly and didn't want to hold me when he was done. Or the way I cried myself to sleep after he left because it wasn't as fun as everyone had told me it would be. What was worse was the part where Kyle showed up.

"I didn't think you were like that, Anika," he told me scornfully.

Then Chris left. And Kyle left. And then somehow Bran left me, too, so I was left all alone.

"No!" I cried. "Don't leave me! I'll change, I'll—"

"Wake up!" Mom was shaking my shoulders. "It's six thirty already!"

A thin layer of sweat covered my body, and my heart was still racing.

"Great," I groaned, keeping my eyes closed.

"Hurry up. You've got to do chores."

I heard her walk out of the room.

After convincing myself it was just a dream and that Kyle already knew who I was and had stuck around, I opened my eyes and rolled onto my side. My phone was charging on the nightstand, and I picked it up to check it.

One new message from Kyle.

Kyle R: Good morning, beautiful.

CHAPTER SEVENTEEN

Dear Anika,

Okay. I have a lot to say to that letter, even though it's probably the shortest one you've written so far. First, I'm going to explain why it took me so long to write you back. My best friend's been getting into something HUGE! I can't say too much, but let's just say he's broken down some major firewalls. Good stuff for the ol' U S of A! We've also been doing a lot of raids, which means I've had plenty of machinery to work on. We actually are making a lot of headway over here, it's just not covered in the news nearly as well as it ought to be. But back to your letter.

I'll admit I don't know you as well as some of your friends and family (though I definitely wish I knew you better, but that will come over time), but I do know you well enough to know I will not decide that I never want to talk to you again. SEEING *someone usually doesn't change that opinion. Even if you ended up sending me a fake picture and turned out to be some weird guy, I would still want to see you. But you're not! Otherwise, I may have to implement some of my military skill on you for lying! Anika, I think all you need is a little self-confidence (sorry if I end up sounding like your guidance counselor). You know you have some really good friends, but you don't think you deserve any of it. Hell, you don't even know WHY you have any of it. If you put yourself outside of the situation, you would realize that the person who made you feel this way—yes, I'm blaming Chris—has a lot of issues himself. The only thing you are guilty of is trusting someone you should have been able to.*

So, Anika, in my last guidance counselor-y act of the day, in your next letter to me, I want you to write down as many positive things about yourself as you can!

Yours,
Shawn

KYLE and I spent the next few days in limbo, and I was having a harder time than ever figuring out what to write to Shawn. Things had been flowing so naturally, but now that he'd asked me to compliment myself, I'd drawn a blank. Usually, it was easy for me to find beautiful things in other people—key words: *other people*—but when it came to me, I was helpless. All I saw were flaws. My nose was a little crooked from when I broke it playing basketball sophomore year. Stretch marks lined my hips from growing so fast in seventh grade. My eyes sat a little too far apart to look natural. My knees were too square and masculine. Not to mention I *hated* it when people were full of themselves. Couldn't Shawn have asked me to write ten positive things about him? It would have made the next letter a whole lot easier.

Every time I thought about my flaws, I almost cried. Maybe if my lips weren't so uneven, Chris would have stayed with me. Or maybe if my voice didn't sound like a whiny little girl's on the phone, I would feel more comfortable talking when people called. It was easier to just have friends and avoid rejection from men. I obviously was unable to tell whether or not a guy actually cared for me... Not to mention, I was the most flawed person I'd ever met, and I'd been receiving enough death glares from Melissa recently to prove I wasn't the only person who thought so.

CHAPTER EIGHTEEN

"ANIKA," Kyle said, after an hour of us doing homework in my room without a single word passing between us. "What's wrong?"

I didn't look up from the question I was working on. Why did it look more like a foreign language than a chemistry problem?

"Nothing," I told him and blinked back tears that had been pressing at my eyelids for hours.

I tried to make sense of the problem again, but kept came up with nothing. Focus, Anika, focus. I chanted to myself. Tears, tears, go away, come again another day.

I felt his finger lightly brush the underside of my chin, and he tilted my face up so I had to look at him. Hadn't he been sprawled out on the bed just a minute ago?

"Please tell me," his voice was very persuasive.

I sighed and prayed the tears wouldn't come. Kyle didn't need to see that. "It's just—" another sigh "—It's just that I've been thinking lately..." My words trailed off because I wasn't sure how to end it correctly.

"About what?" he prompted. His face was solemn to

match the conversation, and his rough hand cupped the right side of my face gently, making me feel protected somehow.

"About... I'm just having trouble finding something good about me."

My voice got all high and whiny at the end of the sentence, and I kicked myself for sounding so pathetic—flaw number 1,243,356.

His face took on a confused look. "Are you serious?"

"Yes!" I cried. The unwanted wetness started flowing down my cheeks. "Why can't I be pretty like Melissa, or smart like Angel, or—"

"Whoa, whoa, whoa. Slow down!" he said.

I took a deep breath.

"Where's this coming from?" he asked.

If I told him about the letter I needed to write, he would have blamed Shawn, so I looked toward my paper-covered desk and shrugged.

"First off, if you can't find anything good about yourself, at least physically, you're looking into a pretty bad mirror. What makes you even more beautiful, and what I love most about you, is your heart."

He'd knelt on the floor beside my chair so we were at eye-level, and took one of my hands into his.

I let my head fall again, because I didn't want him to see me cry, and broke down into heavy sobs that wracked my chest.

"Come here," he said and pulled me onto his knee. Soon, his arms were around me, holding me closer to him, wrapping me in the safe cocoon of his hug. He ran his hand over the hair on the back of my head and kept me close until I finally calmed down enough to talk. Silent tears still poured down my face.

I couldn't believe he was still here. Chris usually ran from emotions or made a joke when things got too serious. Bran usually hugged me and waited awkwardly off to the side for me to soothe myself. Why was Kyle doing this?

"What brought this up?" he asked again.

"I've just been thinking about you, and how Chris was sweet in the beginning, too, and what if..." I couldn't bear to finish. Not just because this wasn't wholly why I was hysteric, but because it was true. What if Kyle did the same thing Chris had done?

The sobs broke through again, and Kyle was shushing me this time.

"Wait, wait—it's okay. Let's just talk about this," he said calmly.

His eyes were wide and trusting, just like—knock it off, Anika! More tears. Why couldn't I just be normal for Kyle? For Shawn? Not this broken down little girl who couldn't even wait until she was on her own to start bawling.

"Okay." I managed to choke the word out.

"There's something I probably should have told you sooner," he said.

I automatically started assuming the worst. He still loved Melissa? Chris was his best friend? He wants to have sex with me?

"What?"

"Here, let's move somewhere more comfortable," he said, and held my hand to help me off his knee. Now I was really worried. Why was he hesitating?

He walked to my bed and shoved his books out of the way, then he sat down and patted the space next to him. I couldn't help but roll my eyes.

He took both of my hands in his.

"What?" I repeated.

"Well," he looked down at the floor, "what Melissa and I fought so much about was sex."

A high-school couple fighting about sex wasn't that revolutionary, especially for people who had dated for as long as Kyle and Melissa had. After every blowup, there were always rumors explaining why they'd broken up—from Melissa cheating, to Kyle being secretly gay, to a silenced pregnancy, to parental interference, and so on.

"What about it?" I asked.

"I told her I wasn't ready yet, and she told me I wasn't much of a man if I didn't want to."

"You guys didn't have sex?" That was the last thing I was expecting. They'd dated for almost three years (barring the intermittent breakups), and the rumor mill had confirmed that they were having sex.

"It's not that I didn't want to—you know, do it—it's just that I didn't want to break the promise I made to God and myself way back in eighth grade. She didn't understand that."

"So, you don't want to have sex?"

It still wasn't registering.

"I won't until I'm married," his voice was soft, and his thumbs were stroking the back of my hands as I looked up at him in wonder.

The Kyle Rayford didn't want to have sex. Wait, I shouldn't say it like that. *My* Kyle Rayford didn't want to have sex. When I realized that, I wrapped my arms around him and kissed him. It was my first kiss since freshman year, but it was so much better. It sent tingles down my spine and fire to my lips. I could have stayed like that with him for hours.

CHAPTER NINETEEN

WHEN I PICKED up a piece of paper and pen to start Shawn's letter, I had a little spurt of writing brilliance but came up short on the positive sides of myself. Even so, I figured something was better than nothing.

Dear Shawn,

The reason it's taken me so long to write back was the "challenge" you gave me last time. I only have a few self-compliments to write to you. I know it's not as many as you asked, but it's a start. Sorry if I let you down, but maybe when you get here, you can help me finish it. Here's my list:

1. *I'm a hard worker*
2. *I have some of the best friends in the world, so I must be doing something right*
3. *My eyes are a really neat shade of blue*

Okay, so short list, but I will work on it! I can't wait for you to come to Roderdale. I am really looking forward to meeting you for the first time in person. I just want to be able to talk to you, and the anticipation is killing me! Hopefully, I will see you soon.

Always,
Anika

I couldn't bring myself to tell Shawn that Kyle and I had turned into a little more than just friends. By doing that, I would also be telling Shawn that there would be no way for us to be together. Not that Shawn had ever told me he wanted to be with me... but soldiers didn't just cross the world to see a pen pal in person. Did they? Would it matter if he did want to be with me?

My heart tugged me in two directions. Kyle was the perfect guy, and I knew I was doing the wrong thing by keeping secrets from him and Shawn. My life was quickly becoming a twisted mess, and I didn't know what to do to prevent it from hurtling toward a disaster. Maybe I did... but I wasn't ready to close either door yet.

CHAPTER TWENTY

THE NEXT FEW days in school were (for the most part) torture. Kyle and I hung out, but between homework, getting things ready for our last month of high school, and starting track season, we were two very busy people. Leslie had been preoccupied with figuring out her student loans because her mom had just told her she wouldn't be helping with expenses for cosmetology school, but Leslie still found it in her to be characteristically overjoyed when I told her about the latest development between me and Kyle. Even though Kyle and I hadn't called each other "boyfriend and girlfriend," Leslie had referred to us as the school's "newest hottest couple" and made her own suggestions about what I could do with Kyle.

Unfortunately, not everyone was as pleased as Leslie. Melissa treated me progressively worse each day. It seemed like she sent me a dirty look every chance she got. She was also surprisingly good at the un-insult, an insult so artfully crafted only she and I knew it was an insult, and if I tried to repeat it to someone else, I would look ridiculous. I was honestly surprised I hadn't finished practice to find my clothes had been stolen or something else equally horrible.

No one in Roderdale knew about all the crap Melissa was pulling except for Bran. After constant begging on my part, Bran had agreed to not tell Kyle or Leslie but was sure to let me know he thought I could beat the living—insert cuss word here—out of Melissa. I loved Leslie, but I couldn't trust her not to spread it around. Besides, she had more important things to worry about. I texted Skye and told her about it, but only because she was from another school and had been through something pretty similar with a girl there.

Barring the words of "wisdom" from Bran and Skye, I was about to snap. In her most outright act of meanness, Melissa had left a note in my locker.

I would give you a condom, but I'm guessing you won't be needing it.

I sighed aloud just as Kyle walked by.

"What is it?" he asked, wrapping his arms around my waist.

I slipped the note in a book.

"Nothing," I lied.

Kyle was too quick. His hand snaked through the air, grabbed the book out of my hand, and opened it to the note.

"What is it?" he teased. "A love letter?"

Kyle held the pink slip of paper, and as he scanned it, the mischievous grin on his face morphed to confusion then anger.

"What the hell is this?" he demanded, holding up the note.

I couldn't bear to look him in the eyes. Kyle never cussed.

"Nothing," I mumbled.

"Nothing?" his voice rose, and I noticed a few people trying to pretend like there weren't staring at us.

I grabbed the note back from him and crumpled it up.

"It's not a big deal," I whispered.

"Where is she?" he asked, his voice just as loud as before.

The crowd in the hallway had started to thin, and I said a silent prayer that Melissa was already in the classroom. I didn't need Kyle to "rescue" me from his ex.

"What's goin' on, Ky?" Miss B. asked, the answer to my prayer. I couldn't help but love her.

"Nothing," he said, shoving his fists into his pockets.

She smiled—albeit disbelievingly—but it was still a smile.

"Good," she said, "because, you're going to be late to class."

I pulled my book out of my locker and started walking into the English classroom. Kyle trailed behind me.

"You know you can tell me about this stuff, right?" he asked.

"Not if it's none of your business," I snapped.

"None of my business? Of course it's my business!"

"Was your name on the letter?"

He grunted in an expression of frustrated caveman I'd never heard before. "Anika, this is crap."

"Just let it go," I said right before we walked into class. The last thing I wanted was for a rumor about our breakup to spread on our first day as the "newest hottest couple."

When we got through the doorway, I froze.

Standing around Miss B.'s desk were three soldiers. One was Shawn Adams, in full uniform.

CHAPTER TWENTY-ONE

I HAD NEVER EXACTLY GONE nuts over men in uniform like the rest of the female population did, but my opinion on that turned 180 degrees the second I laid eyes on Shawn.

He smiled a crooked smile that turned up the corners of his mouth to reveal dazzling white teeth. (They didn't have dentists overseas, did they?) His eyes gleamed with his smile —they were a lot darker today than in the picture.

He easily entered the Top 5 Hottest Guys *Ever* List that I'd been keeping mentally since I was about five. That was saying something when he was ranked amongst men like Matt Damon and Kyle Rayford.

Shawn winked at me.

"Are you going to sit down, Anika?" Miss B. asked.

"Oh. Yeah. Of course," I forced my feet to carry me to my desk and I lowered myself into my chair.

"Okay, now that you're all here," Miss B. said, "we were planning on having an optional recruitment day for you seniors, but your principal thought it would be a best if each of you could hear about some of the sacrifices these brave young men and women are making for their country, especially since you've been writing your pen pals this semester. If you're interested, after class, they can speak with you more about military careers. So, I'll let you guys take it from here."

The oldest of the soldiers nodded, and Miss B. sat down at an empty desk. "So first, we'll just introduce ourselves. I'm Officer Bode Jackson. I work as an MP."

The middle woman took a step forward. "Stephanie Fredricks, Acquisitions."

"Hi, I'm Shawn Adams, Wheeled Vehicle Mechanic."

Bode began explaining the different branches of the military and then the classes of the Army. Each of them told us how they got started in the Army and their job duties. The whole time I couldn't take my eyes off Shawn. Was it a dream?

I felt a tap on my shoulder. For the first time all hour, I looked away from the front of the room and saw Leslie staring at me with her eyes wide.

"Is that Shawn?" she mouthed. I could tell she was holding in one of those squeals she saved for the rare times that something happened involving me and a boy.

I nodded ever so slightly. I didn't need a guy in the military who'd seen and been through so much to see me acting like some love-struck teenager, and I didn't need Miss B. to see and shut the whole thing down.

I looked away from Leslie before we both lost it and directed my attention back to Shawn.

He was one of the most comfortable people I'd ever seen talk in front of a class. The entire time, he kept people interested. (I knew it wasn't just because of his good looks, because when I took time to tear my eyes away from him, the guys in our class were paying close attention, too.) He talked about how it hadn't been his idea to enlist, but his friend, Brady, had talked him into it after they'd graduated from tech school.

By the last five minutes of class, the seniors were asking them questions about the military, and I was pretty sure Shawn had a couple of the guys talked into looking into joining.

The bell rang, and people were still wanting to talk. Me? I was afraid. I'd had the whole hour to stare at him, and now I would have to meet him. What would I say? Should I stay?

Of their own accord, my legs lifted me from the desk, and my feet carried me to the short line of students talking to the soldiers. I stood off to the right a bit so Bode or Stephanie wouldn't try and talk to me.

"Shawn?" I said.

"Hey, Anika." His eyes slowly raked over my body, giving me goose bumps.

It took me a second to locate my jaw and screw it back in place.

"Shawn Adams?" Maybe it still hadn't registered that *Shawn Adams*, my amazing pen pal for the last semester was standing only feet away from me.

His smile morphed into a mischievous grin. "How many do you know?"

Be cool! "A few."

He stuck out his hand for me to shake.

I took it and noticed how rough his hand was—farm hands—and how easily it encompassed mine.

"Nice to meet you," I said.

His hand lingered on mine for a moment. I looked up at him; he stood at least six inches taller than me. Maybe more.

"Hi, Shawn?" Melissa.

Shawn dropped my hand. "Hello."

"Hi, I just wanted to thank you so much for what you do." Never mind the two other people standing there. "And if you'd like, I would love to buy you supper as a thank you for serving our nation."

She slipped him a folded piece of paper, and I was frustrated that no one but me had noticed. I was pretty sure flirting with Army personnel during school broke some sort of rule.

"Well, thank you," he said.

I walked back to my seat and picked up my backpack. I didn't want to look pathetic hanging around for Shawn to talk to me.

Kyle, who I'd forgotten after seeing Shawn, had already left the classroom.

I started walking toward my locker, hoping beyond hope that Shawn would follow me.

"Anika!"

I turned around. It was Shawn.

"Wait up!" He trotted down the hallway to catch up with me.

"Hey," he said, touching my shoulder when his footsteps fell in line with my own.

"Well, you made friends fast," I said.

He snorted. "I couldn't get out of there soon enough."

I kept my smile to myself. Good.

Shawn walked with me as I made the path to my locker.

"So," he said slowly.

"So," I repeated.

I couldn't stop looking at him—I kept glancing sideways just to take him in. There were things I hadn't been able to see in the picture, like the way his dark eyebrows curved slightly upward in the middle.

"What's up?" he asked as I twisted the dial on my locker.

I laughed at the question. It seemed so casual. Nearly a semester of letters, and that's all he had to say? I had so many questions stored up inside of me. So many things I wanted to talk to him about.

"What's funny?" he asked.

I noticed Shawn's grin fall slightly. I turned away to pull a few books out of my locker for the next couple of classes. Great. I was already messing things up.

A small smile had returned to his face again when I turned to look at him. I noticed his dimples this time. I couldn't help but grin stupidly at him.

"Just that you act so casual," I answered slowly.

He leaned against my locker and folded his arms across his strong, broad chest. His grin turned into a smirk in a split second.

"So how am I supposed to act?" he asked.

My head and stomach were doing flip-flops and refusing to work right. What I should have said was something like, "How about you tell me, soldier?"

This is what I said instead: "Uh, well, I—I don't know, I guess."

I *thought* it came out like that. I said it so fast, he had to ask me to repeat myself. It didn't make sense that, out of nowhere, I was nervous and couldn't talk. Hadn't it been only minutes ago that I'd introduced myself to him, cool as a cucumber?

"I guess—" I was interrupted by the late bell ringing.

He smiled again. "Come see me after school?"

That caught me off guard. "Where?"

"I'm staying in a town about half an hour from here...

McClellan," he told me. "I want to spend some time with you."

"Yeah," I said, trying not to sound too eager. "Could you pick me up after practice?"

"Of course," he said. "What time?"

"Six thirty."

He nodded, then he looked me up and down again.

"Anika Anders," he said. "Wow."

I started wondering if my stomach would ever go back to normal.

"I need to get to class," I said, even though I wanted more than anything to stay.

I don't know how it happened, but within seconds, I found myself wrapped in Shawn's arms.

The hug should have been awkward since my backpack was on, but it wasn't. His hands had slipped between the bag and my back, and we were close. My breath caught in my throat. My brain had turned to mush, and now my stomach was in knots. Deep down, I knew there was something I should be remembering, but it stayed at the edge of my mind, out of reach. Shawn kept his arms around me for I don't know how long, then took a deep breath and let go.

"What was that for?" I asked him.

"You thought I was going to let you go without a hug?"

The ability to talk escaped me, but I didn't need to. Shawn turned and moved toward the exit. His walk was straight and proud, but not a march like I would expect of a military man.

"See you at six thirty," he called over his shoulder, and walked out the door.

I smiled to myself and started toward my next class. I was lost in my own personal bliss when I remembered what had been on the edge of my mind—Kyle.

CHAPTER TWENTY-TWO

THE NEXT TWO hours went by slowly and quickly at the same time. My mind replayed my conversation with Shawn, but it also played over every single touch, kiss, and conversation I'd ever shared with Kyle. My heart was heavy, and the knots in my stomach hadn't left, but they weren't the good kind this time.

Every girl asked me a different variation of the same question.

"Who was that guy?"

"Are you going out?"

"Do you two have a thing?"

What I heard was: "Does he live close enough for me to date him?"

"Is he Anika's?"

"Is she cheating on Kyle?"

I was glad when lunch finally came, and I could go sit by Kyle, Leslie, and the rest of the guys, who at least left me alone about it. (Although, Leslie only let it drop on the condition I told her every little detail later that night.)

Kyle was really quiet at lunch. I nudged his arm, and he didn't look at me. I nudged him again.

"What?" he snapped, staring at his tray.

I felt like I'd been slapped. Kyle never talked to me like that, and he definitely was never so dismissive.

"What's wrong?" I asked.

His jaw was clenched. "Nothing."

It obviously wasn't nothing.

"Want to talk about it?" I pressed.

The rest of the guys at the table were starting to look at us. Of course, they were being sneaky about it, peering up while sipping their milk. Leslie was staring openly.

"I said *nothing*, Anika," he repeated, his voice hard.

His words didn't sting as much as his tone, but I let it drop and turned toward Leslie. The confrontation hadn't escaped her notice, and she had a troubled look in her eyes. I shook my head slightly, which I hoped sent the message "don't worry about it." She gave me a weak smile, and I think she understood, because she quickly started talking about a movie set to come out next weekend.

"I don't like slashers," I reminded her.

She had suggested the movie "Murder at Midnight." The title spoke for itself.

She shrugged. "Take Kyle," she said, looking towards him. "Or Shawn," she added in a whisper.

It was my turn to shrug. I didn't want to say that going with Shawn would be preferable to going with Kyle if Kyle kept acting so cold.

After lunch, Kyle put his tray away and walked off without talking to me, but that was fine because I needed to talk to Brandon.

"Can I ask you a favor?" I asked.

"Only if I get one back." He winked.

"I'm serious," I whispered, trying not to let the other people in the hall overhear us.

"Me too."

I punched him on the shoulder.

"Okay! Okay!" he said, putting his hands in the air. "What is it?"

"I'm meeting Shawn after practice tonight—"Bran's eyebrows flew up his forehead "—and I need you to meet me in town and bring me home so my parents don't see him."

If it was possible, his brows lifted even farther. "What?"

"Come on, Bran," I said. "They'd never let me hang out with someone his age."

"There's probably a reason for that..."

"Please. I'll love you forever if you do."

He gave a reluctant smile.

"Welcome to the dark side," he said.

The dark side, I thought. I wasn't doing anything wrong, really. Shawn was a great guy. He was kind, talkative, and selflessly serving our country. My parents should have been completely fine with me dating a guy only a year older than me, especially one like Shawn, but I knew they wouldn't be.

After Chris and I broke up, I spent a lot of time crying. Instead of consoling me, Mom told me that he had "played me like a fiddle" and that I should have listened to her about dating an older guy. The last thing I wanted was to hear more of her "motherly" advice about Shawn.

So, I called her between the end of school and track practice, and she said I could go to a movie with Bran as long as I was back by ten. I was uncomfortable lying, but it really was less stressful for all of us that way.

CHAPTER TWENTY-THREE

AFTER AN EXCRUCIATING TRACK PRACTICE, I still wasn't sure whether I was supposed to be nervous or excited to see Shawn. I showered, and I tried to do my hair and makeup as quickly as possible. When I left the locker room, I saw Kyle sitting on the bleachers outside the door. His hands were jammed in his pockets, and he was looking toward the floor.

"Kyle?" I said, slinging my backpack over my shoulder.

He looked up, his eyes softened, and his face broke into a weak smile. "Can we talk?"

I glanced at the clock. It was already 6:25, and I was supposed to be back by ten. That was only three and a half hours, and with driving time, only about two and a half. How was I going to tell Kyle, my "unofficial" boyfriend, that I couldn't talk to him because I was going to see another guy? Not just another guy, the guy who girls had been swooning over all day.

"Well, I'm kinda—"

He hurried to stand up and interrupted me. "It's okay, it'll be quick," he told me.

My breath caught in my chest. "Okay."

"I wanted to say sorry for how I acted earlier. It's just, I saw the way he looked at you..." He let the sentence trail off. "I just want to let you know that I trust you."

A weight on my heart lifted. "Thank you."

Kyle pulled me into a tight hug and kissed the top of my head.

"Call you tonight?" he asked permission.

"Yeah," he kissed me again on the cheek and left the gym.

I realized that Shawn and I hadn't set a meeting place, but the school was so small there were only a few places he could pick me up. I went to my locker and grabbed one of my books so I wouldn't be awkwardly trailing Kyle outside.

At 6:30, I walked out to the parking lot and looked around.

"Anika."

I looked to my right and saw Shawn, still in uniform, standing next to a white car.

"Hey," I said and started walking toward him.

"Hey," he said.

He walked around the car to the passenger side, opened the door, and took my backpack from me. It struck me that two out of the three guys I'd ever been involved with were true gentlemen... even though I could open a door by myself.

"Have you eaten yet?" he asked when we were both sitting in the car.

"Not yet," I said.

He pulled out of the parking lot and started driving toward McClellan.

"Well, Anika Anders, will you do me the honor of going to supper with me?"

"Of course," I said.

"Why do you say my whole name like that?" I asked as an afterthought.

"Because I feel so lucky that I get to say it," he said.

I looked at the floor mat and blushed.

"So how did you get to be one of the people to come to Roderdale?" I asked after a beat.

He put a finger to his lips. "Brady's a genius."

We talked for the rest of the drive to McClellan, and then Shawn let me pick the restaurant—On the Bricks Café. At suppertime, they lit votive candles for the tables. A restaurant critic would probably describe it as shabby chic, but I liked it because the food was really good, and it was quiet enough for us to talk.

That came in handy, because we filled the better part of an hour with chatter. We talked about everything—his family, where he grew up, what sports he played in school, who his favorite teacher was, what college was like. I told him about my siblings, my parents, school, sports, my best friends. It seemed like there was never a blank space in the conversation until he asked me where I was planning to go to college.

I'd applied and been accepted to a few, but I still wasn't sure where I was going. It had been a point of contention with my parents, and I was having to do extra work to fill out forms for every college. I just didn't know, and I didn't know how to know.

Shawn suggested Upton University because it had a military base nearby. He laughed afterward, but I got the feeling like he was being serious.

He paid for my meal, as well, even though I offered to pay as a "thank you for serving our nation." Okay, I was still a little angry with Melissa.

As we were walking out of the restaurant, he asked me if I wanted to go to the hotel to hang out with him. I agreed, even though this was my first trip to a hotel room with a guy since Chris.

As I followed Shawn up the stairs to his room, I felt as if all eyes were on me. Was the staff thinking bad things about me for being in a hotel with a guy? Would they spread rumors that would somehow get back to Kyle? Before I could get to worrying too much, Shawn opened the door to a room and led me inside. It was a small room. Shawn either hadn't been in there much or had kept it very neat and clean. A plain black suitcase was in one corner, and I saw another, dressier uniform hanging up in the closet.

"Welcome to my room," he said, filling the silence.

I smiled. "It's clean."

Shawn let out a laugh, which I couldn't help but fall in love with.

"Isn't that what people say when they can't find anything else to compliment?" he asked.

I rolled my eyes at him. "So why aren't you telling me I'm clean?"

His face instantly took on a mischievous look. "Well, Mama always said, 'if you can't say anything nice, don't say anything at all.'"

"Hey, I mean it!" I said while playfully punching him on the arm.

Shawn lost the smile and gave me a 'get real' look. "Are you kidding me?"

The conversation had turned serious. While I was struggling mentally to find a way to turn it back light so he couldn't find a spot to tell me something like 'Gosh Anika, I don't know, you're just so... not what I expected,' opened his mouth to talk again, then shut it. I seemed to be walking through mental quicksand, because the more I tried to come up with something witty to say, the more it escaped me.

"You don't have a very good self-image, do you?"

"Maybe just realistic?"

It was Shawn's turn to roll his eyes. "Anyway, I'm pretty sure I could come up with something better to say about you than 'you look clean.'"

"Okay," I grinned. "Shoot."

"Well," he began.

"What, already out of compliments?" I joked, interrupting him.

Shawn narrowed his eyes a little bit while his smile was still in place. It was so cute I wanted to squeal like Leslie.

"No," he replied. "I was going to say, well, you're beautiful for one."

"How original."

"Okay," he said, exasperated. "How about this? Every time you compliment yourself, I'll compliment you, too. Deal?"

I thought it over for a minute. "Deal."

"Okay, start," he ordered.

I saluted him. "Yes, sir!"

"Funny."

I laughed. "Okay, so I'm funny."

Shawn laughed again. "You can't steal sarcastic compliments!"

"Well, I have you laughing, don't I?" I retorted. "So it's your turn."

So I didn't have to face him, I plopped down onto the only bed in the room and looked up at the ceiling. While waiting for him to reply, I counted the little dots in the texture as a way to stop myself from worrying too much.

One, two, three... By the time I got to 20, I got too nervous and moved to my side so I could see him.

He was standing with his hands in his pockets and looking intensely at me. Something about his face indicated that a smart-ass statement wouldn't be the right thing to do at the moment. Instead, I went the serious route.

"What are you thinking?" I asked.

Shawn smiled softly at me. Some people word vomit—well, I brain vomit. Brain vomit is thinking about something entirely random at weird times. At that moment, it dawned on me that Shawn would make a great father someday. He was so smart and kind. With one look, he could communicate that yes, he really cared even though he may not know exactly what to say. (Even so, I guessed being speechless was extremely uncommon for Shawn.)

"I'm wondering where to start," he answered earnestly.

I chewed on the inside of my cheek. Not only was I starting to like Shawn more and more, I was getting closer than I felt comfortable with. I felt a pang of guilt when it dawned on me that it had taken me months to trust Kyle even though I'd known him my whole life. In only an hour I was falling for Shawn, and it was terrifying. The last time I trusted a guy this much— I refused to let my mind wander to Chris and scare me away.

"What's your favorite thing about me?" I asked, shocking myself. Where had that question come from?

"Your smile," he said instantly, his face still serious.

His answer caught me off guard. "My smile?" Why would he like my smile of all things? My teeth were crooked enough to make me self-conscious, but not crooked enough to justify braces. Sure, they were white, but not superstar white. Overall, I thought my smile was one of the most average things about me.

"Yeah," he replied. "When you smile, your whole face lights up. It makes your eyes—I don't even know the word for it... It makes them glow."

"So now my eyes are like those stars little kids stick on their ceilings?" I said sarcastically.

Shawn frowned at me. "Do you realize that when someone starts to get to close to you, you get quiet or crack a joke?"

I didn't say anything.

"Why?" he wondered.

I put my face into one of the pillows and groaned.

Even though I would have liked not to hear, I heard him ask again. "Why do you do that, Anika?"

I shrugged as much as a person can shrug while lying with their face in a pillow.

"Do you not trust me yet?" I could hear the hurt in his voices and I had to answer.

I mumbled a response into the pillow.

"Huh?"

Not wanting to, I rolled over so I was on my back. I still didn't look at him, but instead, resumed counting spots on the ceiling. 22, 23, 24...

"Maybe it's because I don't trust myself," I said.

Shawn moved from where he had been planted with his hands in his pockets to the bed. My breath caught in my chest as I had a vision of Chris peeling off his shirt and crawling into the hotel bed. I instantly shook the memory. Shawn laid down on the bed and shifted to his side so he was facing me. He reached out his hand and drew a line from my shoulder to my wrist with his fingers. My stomach flopped.

Shawn seemed to feel comfortable staring deep into my eyes, but every now and then, looking into his eyes unsettled me. It felt like maybe he was getting too close, seeing too far into me, and maybe figuring out things I didn't want him to know about me.

"Anika," he murmured.

"Yeah?"

He let out a sigh, and his minty breath poured over my face. "Can I try something?"

My heart froze in my chest.

"I—" He closed his eyes and pursed his lips, and I could tell he was going to have trouble saying what he wanted to. "I—"

"Take your time," I breathed.

His eyes were still closed. I was painfully aware of where his hand was on my shoulder and how close he was to me on the bed. As I let my mind wander, the tension built inside of me, and I could feel the electricity flowing between us. It created a magnetic field, pulling me closer and closer to him.

I inched toward Shawn across the comforter. Apparently, he felt the magnetism as well, and he draped his arm over me. His other hand knotted in the bottom of my T-shirt.

"Anika," he whispered in my ear.

Even though Shawn seemed to have found his voice, I had lost mine. Where my heart had frozen before, the beats were now erratic and frenzied. My skin ached to be against his where we weren't touching. Unprepared for this reaction to him, I let out a strangled gasp so quiet I barely heard it.

"I haven't kissed anyone since my ex left me," he said.

The statement and realization of what it meant hit my mind just as it hit my heart. The already hyperactive pattern of my pulse raced ahead. So many thoughts darted around my mind; they were intangible, yet unavoidable. My body knew what to do. I adjusted myself in an effort to close the gap between us.

The smile was gone from Shawn's mouth and in his eyes when I took one final second to look at him before touching my lips to his. His eyes had opened narrowly so he was gazing at me through thick eyelashes.

Maybe Shawn was the one for me. Were Kyle and I supposed to be friends? Too late to decide. I wanted this. Our lips were millimeters apart—

Ring!!! Ring!!! Ring!!!

I moaned. Not now.

"Answer it," he breathed.

Even though pulling myself away from Shawn was one of the hardest things I've ever had to do, I rolled away from him on the bed and retrieved my phone from of my backpack. Without looking at the caller ID, I held it to my ear.

"Hello?" I answered.

"Anika Renee Anders. Where in God's green earth are you?" Mom was pissed.

"I'm just hanging out in McClellan."

I breathed a sigh of relief when she didn't press for further details. "It is already ten o'clock. You better get your ass home right now..."

By the time she was done with her agitated spiel, I had to hold the phone away from my ears. I looked apologetically at Shawn, and the corners of his mouth were pulled down into a frown.

"Fine," I told her. I was eighteen, and I was of the mind that I had a right to decide how late I could stay out. It was only—I looked at the clock—10:05.

"Forty-five minutes," she told me, and the phone went quiet.

"I'll take you home," Shawn offered.

"Wait," said. I went to him and let him wrap his arms around me. "I like this."

Shawn was quiet, but he held me close to his chest. I started comparing Shawn to Kyle but quickly stopped myself. Shawn would be leaving soon. Who was I to think I even got to choose between him and Kyle?

"We should probably go," Shawn sighed into my hair.

He walked me out to the car, which he explained was a rental. I felt bad—and oddly pleased—that he had to pay so much money for this trip. Shawn was here to see me and for no other reason. We kept the chatter up the whole way home, and I couldn't help but appreciate how easy it was to talk with Shawn, and to just be around him. Every now and then, he would look over with a smile on his face and examine me for a little bit. It was unsettling, but at the same time, I liked it.

"Bran's going to give me a ride home," I told him when we got back to Roderdale. "He's going to meet us at the school."

"I could drive you home."

I wasn't about to tell a love interest that he couldn't drop me off at my house because my mommy and daddy wouldn't be okay with it.

"It's fine. Bran already agreed," I said.

"You just want to talk about me on the way home," he said, his smile brightened by the dash lights.

I rolled my eyes but then remembered he was probably looking at the road. "Of course."

He swung the car into the parking lot and turned it off. We were covered in the watery glow from a lone light pole. Bran still wasn't there.

Shawn reached over and took my hand in both of his.

"I knew you were amazing, but I never imagined you'd be this great," he said, stroking the back of my hand.

"You too," I said.

It was true. He'd exceeded every one of my expectations. He was handsome, chivalrous, and forthright about how he felt. Kyle'd asked Bran to invite me to homecoming for crying out loud!

Headlights illuminated the parking lot, and I recognized Brandon's vehicle.

"I guess that's our cue," Shawn said and got out of the car to open my door for me.

"Thank you," I said.

He reached into the backseat and picked up my backpack. I put my hand out to take it from him, but he pulled it away.

"Let me carry it for you."

I didn't point out that Bran had parked a whole four feet away from us.

Brandon got out of his car.

"Hey," he said, his eyes shifting from Shawn to me and back again.

"You must be Brandon." Shawn extended his hand.

"You must be Shawn," Bran said, taking Shawn's hand.

"Nice to meet you," Shawn said. "Anika talks about you —or, I guess I should say wrote about you—a lot."

"Oh, well, you know," Brandon said, "I'm pretty great."

We all laughed, but I noticed Bran didn't really seem happy.

"Well, I need to get back," I said, still burning about my mom's angry call. I wished my parents were as laid back and trusting as Brandon's.

"Nice to meet you," Bran said in an uncharacteristic display of formality and got back into his car.

Shawn walked me to the passenger side and took my hand.

"Thanks for everything," I said.

A charming smile graced his face as he replied. "You're welcome, Anika."

"Can I see you tomorrow?" he asked.

"Of course. What's your number?"

"Hold on," he said and started patting at his pockets.

He found a memo pad and a pen and wrote his number on it. I took it from him and read it... his first letter to me after meeting each other.

Shawn bent down and kissed me gently on the cheek. "Goodbye, Anika Anders."

He opened the door for me and then shut it after I had sat down.

As Shawn walked back to his car, Bran made a motion like he was gagging himself.

"Stop!" I said, looking toward Shawn to make sure he hadn't seen. He was getting into his car, and he waved at us as he drove away.

"Really? What are you *doing*?" Bran asked as he put the car in drive.

I felt a pang of guilt because I knew he was talking about Kyle and me. Of course he had seen Shawn kiss me on the cheek. Still, I didn't want him to know how guilty I felt.

"What?" I put on my seatbelt to avoid looking at him.

I really did value Brandon's opinion. He was my best friend, and—no matter how hard it was to admit—he was rarely ever wrong. Right after he'd discovered Chris had asked me out, he'd told me that Chris was only in it for one thing. I didn't talk to him for weeks after that. Of course, it turned out to be entirely true, and I'd made a point of listening to Bran's frustratingly candid and accurate advice ever since. Even so, I wasn't looking forward to what he had to say now.

"It's just, I saw the way Shawn was looking at you," he started.

I wanted to scream! Hadn't Kyle just said the same thing? I mean, yes, Shawn was older, and I was technically dating Kyle, but I'd been writing Shawn all semester, and he'd come all the way to Roderdale to see me. Didn't that warrant a few dates?

Instead of screaming, I replied in a measured tone. "Where are you going with this?"

He averted his eyes because even though my voice was calm, he knew me well enough to know I was upset. For a second, he was quiet, trying to figure out what to say next without upsetting me, I'm sure.

"Kyle's not going to tell you this. I mean, I know he hasn't even asked you to make it official yet, but he loves you. I don't mean like I love you, I mean he really, truly, deeply cares about you, and it would kill him to see you with someone else." Bran smiled concernedly. "I hope you make the right choice."

"Kyle told me pretty much the same thing after practice."

Bran nodded slowly. "We're just worried about you, and Kyle doesn't want to have his heart broken."

"And you think I do?"

Bran let it drop, and we spent the rest of the ride home talking about the reading assignment in history, but my mind was somewhere else.

Soon enough, Bran had dropped me off at my house,

and I walked to the front door. It was one of those spring nights where the air was cool and smelled like rain. I leaned against the door and shut my eyes so I could replay the evening in my mind. Shawn was so much more than I imagined he would be. My shoulder was still warm from where he'd touched me.

Two and a half years I had been without a boyfriend or even a guy who I regularly went to the movies with (with the exception of Bran, who was most definitely not a love interest). So why was it all of a sudden I had two incredibly wonderful guys in my life? Suddenly, I had to choose between two of the best things that had ever happened to me, and I had no idea how.

I thought about Kyle and me, and my stomach churned with guilt. Shawn had wanted to kiss me, and I was going to let him. I'd *wanted* him to. The night of my first kiss with Kyle out on the trampoline was something out of a fairytale. If I'd never met Shawn, I'd be wanting Kyle to marry me, like, yesterday.

Out of nowhere, the door opened, and I fell flat on my butt.

"What the hell?" I cried without thinking.

When I looked up, I saw Mom standing in the doorway with her hands on her hips. Her blue eyes seemed to be on fire, and her mouth was set in a firm line.

"What took you so long?" she demanded through clenched teeth.

I was still sitting while I tried to figure out how to answer her. The truth or a lie?

"It's only ten thirty." Neither.

"Only ten thirty?" she repeated. I could tell she was starting to get even more wound up. "Just because you're eighteen doesn't mean you get to stay out all hours of the night."

"I came home after the movie," I snapped. "It's one night, and lots of kids stay out way later on school nights."

Wrong answer.

"Not my kids." Her nostrils flared. "And definitely not my spoiled daughter who didn't ask permission to stay out later."

"Look," I said. "I just lost track of time."

I didn't feel comfortable lying to my parents. I hadn't really done much that required lying over the last few years, and when I had lied, the truth had always gotten back to my parents because it was such a small town. Part of me wanted to be close with my mom and tell her all about Shawn, but the other, more logical part of me knew to keep my mouth shut.

"You know that your chores come first," she said. "Now you're going to be up 'til eleven to get them done."

Of course work came first. Work always came first. I just wanted to leave so I wouldn't have to be their unpaid hired hand and wouldn't be constantly pinned under their huge, strict thumbs.

"I'm going to do my chores right now." My voice was tight, and I had to clench my teeth to keep from losing it like I knew I was about to. "Leave me alone."

She started to say something, but I picked up my muck boots and walked out the door before I had to listen to any more lectures.

Outside, I pulled my jacket around me, slipped off my shoes, and pulled on the muck boots. My parents wanted me to check the water for the animals every evening to make sure the floats on the tanks were working. It was a pretty easy job, but I was annoyed that Dad hadn't taken care of it.

I got into the old beater pickup we used to drive around the ranch, and followed the trail to the first pasture. In the roar of the engine, I nearly missed Kyle's call.

"Hey," I said, speaking up over the noise.

"Hey," he said. He sounded timid.

I got to the first tank and turned the pickup off so I could hear him better.

For a few seconds, there wasn't much to hear because we were both trapped in an awkward silence.

"How'd it go?" Kyle finally spoke.

"Good," I said.

I walked over to the tank and saw the water was up and flowing through the float.

"I'm checking tanks," I said.

"Oh, okay."

Was it me, or was he disappointed?

"I'll talk to you later?" I asked, trying to cheer him up.

"Sure."

I dipped my fingers into the cool water and swirled it around.

"Bye," I said.

He didn't say anything back, and I heard the line go silent.

When I got back to the house, it was late and I was exhausted. I tiptoed up the stairs so I wouldn't have to talk to my parents again and slipped into my room. When my head finally hit my pillow, I couldn't get my mind to slow down, so I laid there, waiting to make a decision.

Every touch with Shawn, every word played over and over in my mind like a movie on repeat. It panned to his wide, playful smile and his sparkling, happy eyes. But he was out of high school and in the military. And I was stuck in Roderdale, Texas, about to go to college.

Could I do it? Could I be that Army wife that constantly sacrificed for my husband's career? Could I spend months away from him, not sure if he would ever come home?

Life with Kyle would be so easy, like falling into a play where I knew all the lines. We would go to college together, date a few years, get married, have children, and live happily ever after. He was the sort of steadfast man any woman would be lucky to settle down with.

I tumbled into a restless sleep filled with nightmares. They all had the same theme—wrong choices. After waking up covered in cold sweat and tears several times, I laid back in bed with my eyes open. Slowly, they adjusted to the darkness and I looked around. How could I ever decide?

CHAPTER TWENTY-FOUR

THE DOOR to my room opened and Mom walked in. "Time to get up," she announced.

I looked at my clock: 6:28. Another day, and I hadn't gotten an ounce of restful sleep, *and* it was a Friday. Great.

Even though I was so tired I could have fallen asleep standing up—I carefully picked out an outfit I thought would make me look good. I wore straight-leg jeans, a pair of flats, and a thin black blouse. Whether it was for Kyle, Shawn, or myself, I didn't know.

By the time I was done getting ready, I was late, and Bran was waiting in the driveway.

"Took ya long enough!" he teased, his green eyes lighting up.

I let out a weak laugh. "I know. It's been a hell of a night."

I pulled down the visor and checked myself in the mirror. My eyes looked saggy. I tried to rub under them to get the darkness to go away.

"Stop it," I heard Bran. Before I had a chance to reply,

he said, "I know what you're doing, and stop it. You look fine."

"Thanks."

I laid my head back on the seat and closed my eyes. I had so much to tell Bran, but I was at a loss for words. How could I tell him I was so messed up? Yes, I trusted Brandon. He still was my best friend after I told him and cried to him about Chris. I shared more secrets with him than even Leslie. But I couldn't handle him being disappointed in me.

Instead of having the conversation I knew I could—and should—have had with Brandon, I talked about homework. (While I was so busy feeling sorry for myself the night before, I'd neglected it and now had no clue what was going on.) He told me about the history chapter we were supposed to read. We always helped each other with homework, but usually I was the one helping him. Him helping me... Well, that was a first.

"So what happened was, Russia and the U.S. were like little kids fighting. One of them was like 'I have a bigger bike than you do!' But really, neither of them ever got the bikes out of the garage." Bran's description of the Cold War reminded me why I was the one who always did the helping.

When we got to school, I felt like I had joined the walking dead. My movements were slow and my thoughts even slower.

I saw Kyle in the hallway, and I was anxious to see how he would act after the night before, but he gave me a hug and a small smile, then he said he had to go to a meeting with our principal, Mr. Bougher. He didn't know what it was about but promised to tell me later. Half awake, I hugged him back and shuffled to my locker.

Leslie was there, waiting.

"You look cute!" she exclaimed. "And exhausted," she added as an afterthought.

I scowled at her. "Do you realize that telling someone they look tired is a nice way of saying they look like crap?"

She rolled her eyes at me. When I was tired, I ended up being more of a smartass than usual, and she knew it.

"Hurry up!" she said.

I put in the combination to my locker. When I pulled out my book for English, a fake rose fell onto the floor. Confused as to how a rose got into my locker, I scrunched my eyebrows and stared at it for a moment while my slow-mo brain tried to process it.

Leslie was quicker. She bent over and snatched it up. Without asking—in other words, like a true best friend—she read the card and squealed her signature squeal. Banging my head against the locker would have been less painful than the way that squeal felt against my ear drums.

"Ooh, ooh, read it!" she ordered. I was surprised she wasn't jumping up and down.

I took the rose from her and held the card steady between my thumb and index finger.

I'll care about you until it dies.
Shawn Adams

The smile I thought would be impossible to have found my lips and wouldn't go away. I held the rose in my hands for a few seconds longer while some of the girls passing by in the hallway stared on in either jealousy or curiosity. (With the exception of Melissa, who still hated me. She just glared.)

Leslie's excitement was something I felt rather than saw. No, the only thing I had eyes for was the fake rose.

Shocking me out of my stupor, the bell rang, loud and shrill. I placed the rose on a shelf in my locker and hurried off to Miss B.'s class, thankful that she was really the one (with her assignment) that got this beautiful mess started. Of course, I couldn't be too grateful when she chided Leslie and me for our tardiness.

"Okay, so I know we're nearing the end of the year," she began, earning a few whoops from the seniors, "but I have one assignment left." Groans replaced the previous cheers.

"It's not going to be that bad, but it will require some thinking on your part. What we are going to be doing is difficult and will take time, which I know you're pressed for, but I want a quality piece for your last paper. Okay?"

The class murmured, and Bran leaned up to whisper in my ear. "Anika, wanna have a study date?" I could almost see him winking cheesily at me.

"Almost as much as I'd like to go skinny dipping in Alaska."

Miss B. kept talking through our banter. "Every teacher thinks their class is important, but now that you're about to graduate, I think I can tell you that this will be the most important assignment of your high school careers. You're going to write a thank you note to your pen pal. I will read this letter, because I really want it to be good. Any questions?"

Melissa's hand shot into the air like a firecracker. "Isn't that an invasion of privacy?"

Miss B. shrugged. "Think of it as quality control."

There were so many things that I wanted to thank Shawn for, none of which I would feel comfortable having a teacher read.

"Anyone else?"

When no one asked her a question, she said, "Okay, first I want you to write a list of what you're thanking them for. That will be your basic outline. Raise your hand when you're done so I can see everyone's before class is over."

"Are you allowed to thank Shawn for that rose?" Leslie whispered to me.

I snorted. "That would go over well."

"Girls!" Miss B. said from her desk. "Be. Quiet!" She stressed each word, making it sound like its own sentence.

Without response, Leslie and I started working on the list. Several boys had their assignment done within minutes (which Miss B. made them add to), but it took me a little bit longer to write down appropriate items. After about twenty minutes of hard work, I raised my hand, and Miss B. walked to my side.

She looked over my shoulder and was quiet for a minute before talking.

"I like it," she finally said and moved on to one of the other students who had their hand raised.

Leslie walked with me to our next class.

"Are you going to see him tonight?"

We both knew she was talking about Shawn.

"Yeah, but my mom's mad at me. I don't know if she'll let me go out."

"Just tell her you're staying at my house," Leslie suggested.

She was so cavalier about it that it took me a minute to process it.

"Can I actually stay at your house?"

I wasn't about to show up at the house at two in the morning and try to explain why I wasn't at Leslie's.

"Yeah, my mom won't care."

Between the next couple of classes, I texted Shawn and my mom and set up the plans. Mom said I could stay at Leslie's on the condition that I took one of my sibling's chores the next day. Shawn said he would pick me up after practice.

CHAPTER TWENTY-FIVE

I FINALLY SAW Kyle again in algebra, but our teacher had everyone so stressed about the impending final exam that we didn't have time to do anything but write down the equations on the board for practice. Though we didn't get to talk, I could tell Kyle was happy about something. At lunch, I got to ask him what it was.

"I'm valedictorian!" he said. "And there's something about you—"

"Miss Anders?" Mrs. White, the school secretary was standing behind me. "You need to visit the principal's office when you're through with lunch."

"Okay," I replied, but she was already walking away, followed by the clacking sound her high heels made on the hard floor.

A smile was blooming on Kyle's face.

"What?"

He shrugged, still smiling. "I guess I won't have to tell you anymore."

"Aww, please!"

He shook his head.

"Pretty please."

"Nope."

"Come on. You know I hate surprises!"

He grinned and shook his head. "I think you'll like this one, though."

"Well," I said, exasperated. "I guess I better go find out!"

I picked up a roll to take with me and left my tray—Kyle always ate what I didn't finish anyway.

He smiled again. "See you later, An."

I bent down and kissed him on the cheek. "See ya."

The walk to the principal's office was quick enough. Suspense for what was going to happen built up inside of me. Kyle made it sound like it was a good thing I was going, but I couldn't stand our principal. Mr. Bougher was one of those guys who was smarter than average and was sure to let everyone know. He'd probably become principal just so he could lord over generations of students.

Before entering his office, I took a deep breath to gather myself. Then, I knocked lightly on the door and walked in.

"I was supposed to see you?" I said.

He smiled and pointed at the chair across from his desk. "Yes. Sit down."

I did as he asked in silence and waited for him to say more.

"Do you know why you're here?"

"No."

Of course I didn't know. If I knew, I wouldn't be sitting in his office.

"Well, with graduation coming up, I think it's time to tell you the good news."

"Good news?" Why couldn't he just tell me?

"Very good news," he confirmed.

I waited for him to share the "very good" news, but he just smiled wanly and looked at me with watery blue eyes.

Quit beating around the bush! "Well... What is it?"

"You are the class salutatorian."

"Salutatorian?" I tried to say, but it came out like a squeak.

"Now I'm guessing you know that Kyle's valedictorian of your class?"

"Yes." My voice sounded a little bit better this time.

"Well, you two are going to be..." He filled me in on all of my responsibilities as salutatorian. First, that meant that even though I was ranked high in the class, I still needed to do well for the last couple of weeks because, otherwise, he could strip my title from me. (It was hard for me not to roll my eyes at that.) Next, I would be giving a speech "no shorter than five minutes but no longer than eight minutes" at graduation. The speech was to include fond memories, thank yous, and anything else I felt like adding in. (Could he just write it for me?) It was to be written by myself. (Oh really?) And I couldn't have help from parents or teachers.

"Okay," I told him and walked out of his office, still not sure how to feel about the whole thing. Kyle seemed to be happy for me, though.

He'd saved an empty seat for me in computer projects, and I shared the "good news."

"Told you you'd like it," he said with one of his most breathtaking grins.

His face was glowing with pride, but I didn't have the heart to tell him that I *hated* making speeches. Talking in front of pretty much the entire population of Roderdale didn't sound appealing to me. Actually, it was about as appealing as a pan of deep fried worms.

"Yeah, you did," I agreed with a—hopefully—convincing smile.

He squeezed my arm and then bent over the project he was working on. I sneaked a peak at the headline on the document he had open: Valedictorian Speech. It was then I realized how much Kyle had wanted this. He was easily one of the hardest working kids in my class (which I might mention had a whopping total of twenty-four kids), and I knew he was going to carry on his work ethic with him after graduation. He'd told me a few days ago that he was going to attend college at Upton University and would be playing basketball there, though he hadn't revealed that bit of news to anyone except family. My heart swelled with pride for Kyle. How could I hurt someone as honest and hard-working as him?

I made it through the rest of the day, but by the end, I felt even more exhausted and slow-moving than when I'd started. Track practice would be a pain, and we only had a week before regionals. The chances of me making it to the state competition were slim, so I had even less motivation to actually go to practice, let alone try when I got there.

Of course, track practice was more demanding than I had previously expected. Every time I lifted my foot for more distance, I felt like my shoes were made of cinder blocks. Every pushup felt like I was pushing the world down instead of myself up.

When the practice was finally over, I staggered to the locker room and showered. All of the other girls had left by the time I got done, and it was nice to have the locker room to myself. I could finally think without being interrupted with questions about my love interests or hearing about other peoples' petty drama. Didn't they know people had actual problems to worry about?

The extra time didn't help me, though, and I was just as mixed up as I was before, but I did know Shawn wasn't going to be here forever, and I was going to see him tonight while I still could.

When I exited the locker room, I almost ran into Kyle. He was standing with his backpack over his shoulders and his thumbs in his pockets. For the first time today, I noticed what he was wearing: a navy blue, long-sleeved button-up shirt with jeans, boots, and a brown belt. It surprised me a little bit—I hadn't seen him dress country for a while, but I realized I liked it; it suited him.

"Hey," I said, leaning into his hug.

"Hey. Do you have a minute?" he asked.

"Sure."

Kyle took a step back and I realized he was holding a rose in his hand... at the same time he realized I was doing the same.

"What's this?" he gestured at my hand.

Not for the first time today, I was at a loss for words.

He gingerly took the fake rose, flipped the card over, and read it. The smile slipped from his face just as easily as it usually came, and his skin took on a pallid tone. All the lights in his usually bright brown eyes had left, leaving them dull and listless.

"Oh," he said.

Before I knew it, both roses were on the ground, and Kyle was striding away.

I was standing there. Unable to move.

"Kyle!" his name escaped my lips in a croak, but it was already too late. The heavy metal gym door banged shut, and I was left staring at the empty gymnasium.

I let my backpack fall to the floor as I sagged to my knees. With tired, shaky hands, I picked up the roses and read the card attached to the soft red rose that Kyle had meant for me.

Roses are red,
violets are blue.
I want you to be my girlfriend,
and I hope you do to.
Love, Kyle

A lump grew in my throat, and I blinked back tears. Why did he have to do this to me? Didn't he know I loved him? That he taught me how to trust again? That he was the only person besides Brandon who would listen to me cry about Chris and not chastise me for trusting him in the first place? That he was my everything?

Why did this have to be so hard? I wondered. Did love stories always go this way, or would mine turn out to be a tragedy? Panic quickly wrenched my gut as I realized maybe neither of them would want me in the end. It would figure. Just like Chris, I would feel happy and in a love that seemed like it would last, and then out of nowhere, the rug would be pulled from under me, and I would be left even more miserable than before. My already fragmented heart would shatter into pieces that would become harder and harder to pick up.

I couldn't keep doing this to myself.

Don't cry, I ordered myself like a drill instructor. Stand up. Somehow, I found my way to my feet, then wiped a few stray tears that had disobeyed orders. I could handle this. I could handle everything. I was Anika Anders. But somehow, my affirmations didn't sound too convincing.

I picked up my backpack off the floor and walked out of the gym to see Shawn. He was waiting for me.

CHAPTER TWENTY-SIX

WHEN I SAW Shawn in the parking lot, I fell just as easily into his arms as I had with Kyle only moments earlier. All that mattered was him, me, and the steady beat of his heart. He kissed the top of my head and rubbed my shoulders before letting me go.

"I know this is fast, but I missed you, Anika."

The blue-green of his bright eyes and my own mixed emotions kept me imprisoned for a moment.

"I missed you, too," I finally said.

"So, what do you want to do?" he asked.

"Let's cruise," I answered and handed him my backpack.

He raised an eyebrow. "Cruise?"

"What? Are you too old to cruise?" I asked, forcing my tone to stay light.

Shawn reached out and caught a lock of my hair.

"Your hair's curly," he said. "I didn't know that."

I had a flashback of Kyle telling me the same thing.

"I don't like it," I admitted. "I usually straighten it or something."

"It's beautiful."

Not knowing what to say, I blushed and got into the car.

He shut the door for me and walked around the front. I appreciated the chance to watch him. He was out of uniform today, wearing pale, faded jeans and a white T-shirt that stretched over his biceps. I noticed the blue ink of a tattoo peeking below the hem of his sleeve.

"So, cruising?" he said when he got in.

"Let's take a dirt road," I said.

To be fair, there were only a handful of paved roads in Roderdale, but I wanted to show him my slice of Texas.

I directed him out of town, toward a pasture that I knew no one would be driving by so we could have some privacy. He maneuvered the car to the side of the road and parked. It was warm, so I opened the door and got out.

Texas was beautiful. A breeze made the yellow grass on the rolling hills wave like a golden ocean. Black cattle dotted the pasture and dark brown specs in the sky showed birds in flight. The sky had an orange tinge to it that always came before sunset.

I sat on the ground next to Shawn with his thick shoulder brushing my thinner one. Electricity crackled between the two of us, and I felt my breathing hitch and my pulse quicken. I hated the way he put me on edge, but part of me loved the feeling.

I looked over at him and saw him staring at me with a burning intensity I'd never seen from a boy before. It struck me how much older he was than me, despite only being nineteen. He had seen and done so much. That experience seemed like such a large number in my mind but so small when we were sitting this close.

I reached up and cupped his cheek.

Shawn took my hand in his and held it to his muscled chest.

"Do you feel that?"

Knowing he meant his heartbeat, I answered quietly, "Yes."

If he felt my pulse, would he feel the pain that throbbed with each beat? Would he know the struggle I was facing? Would he understand? What would he think? What would he do if he were in my situation?

So many questions with no answers. So many questions I was too cowardly to ask. So many questions that I needed to ask. Images of Kyle running away flashed through my mind... and I was here.

"Shawn, I've got to go," I said before he could enchant me and unknowingly entice me to stay.

"What?" his brow furrowed together. "Why?"

"My parents want me home," I lied.

Looking juvenile to him would be better than admitting the truth.

I stood up, brushing broken pieces of grass from my pants.

"Okay," he said.

He took my hand in his and led me to the car. I relished the feeling, knowing it could be the last time he touched me like that. Before he opened the door, he leaned me against it.

"Something's up," he said.

I couldn't deny it, so I didn't say anything.

"Anika..."

He rested his forearm where the door met the hood and looked at the ground.

Like an instinct, I reached out and hooked a finger

through his belt loop. My thumb brushed against the soft skin over his hip.

He looked down at me and inched closer. His eyes were dark, confused.

"Is this it?" he asked.

"I don't know."

We both knew it was.

Then he closed the gap. His hands cupped against my face, and our eyes locked. It was the most intimate I'd been with another person.

"Can I kiss you?" he asked. "Just once."

His thumb traced over my cheek to my bottom lip. I closed my eyes and took in his scent. It was overwhelming.

"Yes," I said.

And his lips were crushing mine. Every bit of him was against me. I ran my hands over his sides, touched his arm where I knew his tattoo was, felt the invisible stubble on his chin.

He pressed against me and held me to the car. His lips poured over my mouth, my cheeks, my neck. It was desperate, exciting, longing—a representation of the relationship we could have had. Our first and last kiss.

We broke apart and looked at each other for a long moment.

His eyes searched my face. For what, I wasn't sure.

He reached beside me and opened the door.

I got in.

He drove me to the school parking lot so I could get my vehicle. When he opened the door for me and I got out, I had to fight back tears. Without waiting for his reaction, I hugged him, and his arms slipped around me. I tried to remember everything about how it felt.

"When are you leaving town?" I asked.

"I'm going home tomorrow."

"Thank you," I choked out. "For everything."

He kissed the top of my head.

"Anika Anders."

"Shawn Adams."

He kissed me on the cheek. "Goodbye."

CHAPTER TWENTY-SEVEN

AFTER SHAWN HAD DRIVEN AWAY, I called Bran.

"Are you okay?" he asked after hearing my voice crack. "What's going on?"

Sitting in my pickup with tears in my eyes and my phone pressed against my cheek, I explained to him about seeing Kyle after practice and telling Shawn goodbye. I turned on my pickup and started driving. Soon, pastures on the outside of town were blurring by.

"What are you going to do?" he asked.

"I've got to see him."

My house passed through my peripheral vision. Five minutes later, I was parked behind Kyle's family's tree row.

Now that I was there, I wasn't sure what to do.

"I'm here," I said.

"His room's around the right side," Bran said quietly.

We both knew that I knew where Kyle's room was. Bran was just giving me an extra push.

I chewed on my bottom lip.

"It'll be okay," he said through the phone. "Just go."

I got out of my pickup and walked to the right side of

the house. Through the front windows, I saw his parents sitting in the living room. His bespectacled dad had a newspaper spread in front of him on the coffee table. His mom had her feet tucked under her while she watched something on the television.

The sky was fairly dark, so I wasn't worried about his parents seeing me, but I still kept my head down as I crept around the house to his room.

He was sitting at his desk with his head in his hands. He used one hand to roughly pull his shirt up and wipe at his face. I felt like an intruder. Kyle's emotions were raw, open, and sincere.

Love. The word came to my mind. I loved him.

"Kyle," I said.

He didn't hear me.

I tapped at the window, and he looked up and saw me.

For a moment, his face was entirely blank with shock. Then, I watched the change in his face as the hurt returned. He was trying to mask how much he was suffering, but I knew. I understood. I felt it, too, for causing him so much grief.

We stared at each other for I don't know how long. His eyes finally hardened. With one simple gesture, he nodded, spun his chair again, and fought off sobs.

"Kyle!" I said again, louder this time.

He didn't look at me, but instead, I saw his shoulders shake with the force of his efforts.

"Kyle!" his name became my song, my cry, my plea.

Tears mirroring his smarted in my eyes, and I found it hard to stand with this wall of wretched pain between us.

"Please, Kyle, come outside," I said. I knew he could hear me, even though he wasn't facing me.

Finally, he turned around, got up, and walked over to

his window. Too slowly, he pulled the screen out, and stepped into the night with me.

"Please," I begged. One word, and he knew.

A grimace broke out on his face as took me into his arms. Kyle cried openly now, but I could tell they were tears of relief instead of those horribly painful tears. For a second, I let him hold me while the rivers on his cheeks subsided. I rested my face against his chest and took in his sweet scent.

"I love you, Anika."

At first, I didn't believe he'd said it.

Bran was right... he truly, deeply loved me. I felt a familiar swoop in my stomach, and warmth spread through my chest. Kyle loved me.

Kyle loved me *back*.

All of my doubts about my choice were buried by the sense of utter peace and love that encased me whenever Kyle and I were with each other.

Shawn was an amazing guy. He was beautiful and kind and honest. Some girl would meet Shawn someday and make him feel so much love his heart would burst. The thought of losing her would tear him apart just as the thought of losing me had torn Kyle apart.

Right now, Shawn had only a very small portion of my mind. For the most part, I was looking at Kyle. His cheeks were bright, and his eyes were swollen from crying.

"I love you," I said.

Kyle gave me a slow kiss, wet from tears. When he was done kissing me, he smiled lovingly down at me and used his thumbs to wipe the wetness from my face. I'm sure I looked a mess—mascara streaking down my face and the whole nine yards—still, Kyle said to me, "You're so beautiful."

"Thank you," I breathed and melted into his arms for another long hug.

CHAPTER TWENTY-EIGHT

"THANKS FOR COMING," I said.

Shawn had agreed to meet me for breakfast before he left, and we were sitting in my favorite diner in McClellan.

"Of course," he said, but there was no warmth in his voice.

A middle-aged waitress came and asked us for our drink orders, and we made some small talk until she came back to ask us what we wanted to eat. After she waddled away, I took a deep breath.

It was now or never.

I reached into my purse, pulled out an envelope, and handed it to Shawn.

His head tilted to the side a little. "Anika, you didn't ha—"

"Just read it," I said. "Please."

He took the envelope from me and started peeling back the flap.

"Miss B.'s having us write our soldiers a thank you letter, but I wanted to give you the real one first."

He pulled out the sheet and held it in front of him.

Dear Shawn,

I'm sorry. I don't think I'll ever be able to tell you enough how absolutely sorry I am. I'm guessing by now you know the reason I left you was because there's someone else: Kyle. I wanted to tell you it's not that I don't love you, it's that I love him. I haven't told anyone this yet, not even Kyle, but I think he's the one I'll be with for the rest of my life. I hope he wants me for the rest of his life as well.

I don't want to tell you that our relationship would never have worked, but it would have been very difficult. Stress would have been high, and can you imagine how awful it would be after seeing each other knowing that would be the last time possibly ever. It would have crushed me. You wouldn't have been able to focus when you went overseas, which would have put you in even more danger.

We've only been around each other for two days, and I have already felt so many things... uncontrollable passion with you. Someone told me once that if you meet a guy and he makes you uncomfortable—sets you on edge, is irresistible—run away. We burn too hot, and I would never want us to burn out. Not to say that you aren't a great guy, because I believe with all of my heart that you are.

Someday, you will meet a girl. She will be gorgeous, funny, smart, understanding, talkative, all of the things you love, and she will steal your heart. Unlike your last girlfriend, she will take care of it. She'll cherish the love that you give her, and most importantly, she'll never let you go like I'm about to.
Shawn. Thank you so much for everything you've done for

me. I hope we can still be "Pen Pals" (I put quotes around that, because you are so much more to me than a pen pal), but I will understand if you are unable, or unwilling. Again, I'm sorry.

Love,
Anika

Watching him read what I'd written was one of the hardest things I'd ever done. Part of me wanted to rip the letter from his hands and kiss him like we had the night before. The more logical part of me knew better.

He set the letter on the table, looked toward the ceiling, and blinked a few times.

"So, this is how you really feel?" he asked. Shawn wasn't angry or bitter or mean, he was just asking the question.

"Yes."

I put my napkin over my face to hide my tears.

"Come here."

I stayed planted where I was. I knew if I got up and went to him, I would lose the small bit of resolve I had left. So, Shawn got up and slid into the booth with me. He embraced me, and I cried into his shoulder.

"I'm sorry," I bawled. "So sorry."

"Hey," his voice trembled. "Once a pen pal, always a pen pal."

As I watched Shawn drive away, I couldn't help but wonder how I'd altered my life with my decision. I didn't know if or when I would ever see him again. I only knew that being friends would be too hard so soon. I just hoped that the letter I'd given him wouldn't be the last letter of mine that he'd read.

CHAPTER TWENTY-NINE

"HIGH SCHOOL HAS BEEN... like nothing I've ever expected," I began my salutatorian speech in front of almost the entire town of Roderdale.

"Over the last four years, I've learned things, experienced things, and enjoyed things I'd never knew I could..."

"You did great, An!" Kyle picked me up and spun me around after we walked out of the gym.

"Careful!" I said tipping my mortar board back. "This thing could take an eye out!"

Mom and Dad came and hugged me.

It was over. I couldn't believe it, but it was over.

After the reception was finished, I went home so I could be alone in my room. In an effort to calm my mind, I started packing. Kyle and I would be going to Upton in only a month, since football practices started early, and Mom had picked up some boxes for me. I hung up my cap and gown and set the tassel on my nightstand. Then I pulled open the drawer and saw all my letters from Shawn. I ran my fingers over one of the envelopes.

He'd sent me one last letter in response to the thank you letter Miss B. had us send.

Dear Anika,
Thank you so much for the letter. You really are something special. I wish you all the best in your future. You deserve it.
Yours always,
Shawn

I held the paper to my chest and closed my eyes.

CHAPTER THIRTY

"ARE YOU ABOUT READY?" Kyle asked me after loading the last of my bags into the back of his pickup.

"Almost." I smiled at him. "One second."

I ran to where my family was waiting on the porch. Mom was teary-eyed. I said goodbye and hugged the people I'd grown up with for the last eighteen years.

"It's been quite a ride, hasn't it?" Dad asked.

I nodded, not trusting my voice to speak.

Kyle shook hands with my parents.

I got into his pickup and buckled up. As we drove down our country road with dust billowing behind us, Kyle asked, "Are you ready for the rest of our lives?"

I looked at him and smiled. "As long as it's with you."

Thank you for reading Anika Writes Her Soldier! Want to see Shawn get his happily ever after? **Read the alternate ending**!

Stay in Anika's world a little longer with Chasing Skye. You can **get the complete series bundle for 50% off** when you support Kelsie directly!

CHASING SKYE

SNEAK PREVIEW

CHAPTER ONE

KELLUM WATTS BURST through the door, parting his lips in an apologetic grin. "Sorry I'm late!"

"The first day, Kell?" the teacher asked. "Not a good way to start out."

"I know," he smiled again, shaking his damp brown hair around his face, and Mrs. Valor practically melted into a pile of blushing, Kellum-loving goo. "It won't happen again."

Every line that formed around his eyes when he smiled etched itself permanently into my memory. No dimple left behind.

He slid into an empty seat reserved especially for him between Saffron and Zack. Saffron reached out and scratched Kellum's shoulder with her French-tipped nails. Kellum matched her adoring smile with one of his own and hooked the strap of his backpack over his chair, then scanned the room.

His brown eyes met mine.

I looked down at my notebook.

"Well, now that everyone's here, we can get back to class," Mrs. Valor said.

She continued with the first-day speech teachers gave every year, which usually included a syllabus and the word "respect." Between wondering if Saffron could smell his cologne and fretting about volleyball tryouts, I barely caught a word.

The bell rang, and I retreated to the hallway, not wanting to see if Kellum would carry Saffron's books.

"Hey, Skye!" Kylie appeared beside me.

I jumped, putting my hand over my heart. "You scared the crap out of me."

She laughed and shrugged. "How was A&P?"

"It was okay," I replied without asking how she already knew my class schedule. In two years of knowing her, I'd learned to just go with it and enjoy her uncanny knowledge of everybody's business. "What classes do you have?"

"Oh, this and that. We have English and history together."

The warning bell rang, and she waved goodbye before veering off down a different hallway. I took my time walking to Spanish where I found Señora Luna standing in front of a full classroom wearing a gaudy sombrero.

For the next hour, she gave us the cultured version of Syllabus Day ("*¡Respeto!*") and then I made my way to the free reading period. I suffered through Mr. Winkel's nasally reminder to read a book and write a report every quarter before the bell finally rang and I could go to weights class.

The gym lights were off as I walked down the sideline to the girls' locker room, but light from the windows shined on the volleyball net. Excitement crackled through my muscles and danced over my skin. New year, new volleyball season, new position, new me.

I stepped down the stone stairs to the dingy locker room and saw Rachel and Shelby were the only other girls there. Both of them were on the volleyball team with me the year before, so I figured we'd be a good group.

We talked about our summers and volleyball tryouts, then headed back to the gym.

Coach Rokey waited for us in the corner by the door. About fifteen guys already circled around him, and I hoped Kellum would be in the group. When we got closer, I heard his laugh before I saw him. It brought a smile to my lips.

Rokey used his finger to count everyone out. "Okay, follow me."

We walked through halls, giving me a better view of Kellum. His shirt sleeves were cut off so low I could see the muscles work in his shoulders as he walked.

Coach Rokey led us to an open area in the weight room, and Kellum stopped in front of me. He must have grown over the summer because he stood several inches taller than my 5-foot-six frame.

"You'll be in groups of three according to ability," Rokey told us. "Girls, you'll go together. Kellum, Bryant, Kaiser, you're a group..."

After sorting us into groups, Rokey had us bench press. Shelby barely managed 75 pounds. Rachel followed at 105. When my turn came, Coach joined our group to spot me. I'd been nearing the record of 120 pounds all summer, but I was about to press 125.

Laying on the bench, I stared up at the bar, wrapping my hands around the cold metal. Feeling every bit of the weight, I lifted it from the rack, lowered it to my chest, and started the slow push up. My arms froze, elbows bent, and I struggled to get past the stall in my lift.

"Come on!" Rokey urged.

Grunting out a breath, I broke past the invisible stop and pushed the bar all the way up for one rep. I racked the weights, making a satisfying clang of metal on metal.

Coach grinned down at me. "This is what you get for coming to summer weights!"

I'm sure my face was all sorts of red and unattractive as I sat back up, grinning.

Zack slapped me a high five. "Nice!"

I blushed, thankful for the cover of exertion. Sure, I wanted Kellum's best friend to recognize me, but not especially for bench press.

"Embrace it," Rokey said. He must have caught the blush.

Shrugging, I tried to make my face normal. Thankfully, Rokey released us to go change, and I didn't have to stand around the rest of the boys much longer. I caught Kellum looking at me on the way back to the gym, but he was probably just surprised about the record.

The guys and girls split at the gym entrance, and we made our way toward the locker room.

My arms ached as I struggled to change out of my gym clothes. "I'm gonna be sore tomorrow," I said, groaning.

"Man, I wish I could lift like that," Rachel said.

"Yeah," Shelby said, "but too much muscle slows you down in volleyball anyway."

I jerked my head back, shocked. Was she being serious?

"What do you mean?" Rachel asked, reading my mind.

"The college coach I talked to this summer at camp said he'd trade speed for power any day." Shelby cast me a sideways glance. "Bulky girls are just slower."

I could practically feel the cold cement floor on the underside of my jaw. She had to be kidding.

"You have to have power to hit," Rachel shut her locker. "And serve."

"That's just what the coach told me." Shelby sat down and started knotting up her shoelaces.

I remembered the college where she went to the camp. A division two, nobody school.

"What was their record last season?" I asked, trying not to let her comment make me regret all the hours I spent in the weight room over the summer.

Shelby looked at me finally, her eyes narrowing once she realized what I meant. "This coach came from Upton, 32-1 last season. But don't worry, Skye. There are lots of bigger girls on community college teams."

Shelby shut her locker, smiled at me, and flounced away.

I ground my teeth, mad at what Shelby said and madder I let Shelby have the last word.

Rachel opened her mouth, "I—"

I shook my head.

"But—"

I raised my hand. "That doesn't even deserve a response."

I tried to believe that lie, but I couldn't. The truth was, it stung, especially coming from a senior.

Rachel and I made small talk while we finished changing and then headed to the cafeteria. We were lucky enough to fall in line a few people behind Kellum and Zack.

Kellum looked straight at me. "Hey, what was the record before, Skye?"

It took me a minute for my brain to connect with my mouth. "Um, 120, I think."

"Cool. Good job," he said and turned back to Zack.

An insuppressible smile stretched my lips, and it lasted

for a full five minutes until I saw Shelby at the table. Most of last year's volleyball team sat together, and I took a seat as far away from her as I could.

Volleyball tryouts dominated the conversation. Tryouts at McClellan weren't really tryouts. Since it was a smaller school, everyone got to be on the team, but we did have to fight for playing time in the positions we wanted.

Kylie waved her carrot stick around as she talked. "You know me. Middle hitter, all the way."

"Same," Rachel said, shrugging. She'd played the spot for the last three years. Trying out was just a formality for her at this point.

Just as I opened my mouth to talk, Shelby told everyone she wanted to be libero, meaning she'd get to wear a special jersey and play back row the entire game. She thought it would give her a better chance at playing in college the next year.

A few of the girls told her she would be great for the position.

I kept my mouth shut.

The second half of the day passed much the same as the first half.

English, "r-e-s-p-e-c-t."

American History, "Remember the Alamo?"

Calculus, "The limit on a bad attitude *does* exist."

Journalism, "Being a good journalist is about more than the quality of your work."

Of course, everyone would forget the whole good-attitude thing less than a week in—including the teachers—and school would be back to normal.

What I'd been looking forward to all day finally came: the final bell. I threaded my way through the throng of students rushing to get home and made it to the locker room, changing in record time.

I had on my favorite kneepads along with spandex, a cutoff T-shirt, and a pair of broken-in volleyball shoes. Within fifteen minutes, I had stretched and was practicing my serve.

"Ladies!" Coach Umber's voice rang throughout the gym. "Take a seat at center court."

The rest of the girls and I jogged over and sat in a semicircle under the net facing Coach and Tasha Wilkens, the assistant coach. For the first ten minutes, Coach took roll and asked us which positions we would like to try out for, jotting notes on a clipboard.

When she called my name, I tried to sound confident. "Libero."

I didn't dare check Shelby's expression. The other girls' poorly hidden looks of surprise said all I needed to know.

Shelby'd already said she wanted the position at lunch, and since she was a senior, I was supposed to back down and say "defensive specialist" or "outside hitter" and wait for next year to have my turn.

I just couldn't do it. If Coach thought Shelby was better than me, I'd take a different spot, but I knew what I wanted, and I wanted to be varsity libero.

Coach nodded like nothing potentially disruptive to the accepted social order had happened and called on the last of the girls. After that, she had us do some warm-ups and then ran us through several drills. The practice wasn't overly difficult and wasn't anything compared to what regular season practices would be like, but I still worked up a sweat.

Being back on the court felt like heaven. On the court was the only place I could let my mind go and let the rhythm of the game take over. Volleyball made sense in a way the rest of life never did, and I liked the way I fit into the game.

I wasn't sure where I stood compared to Shelby, but I out-hustled her every chance I got, and I was sure Coach would notice that.

In the locker room after practice, the atmosphere was different than other year's post-tryouts scene. Usually a couple of girls were frustrated with their performances and complained, best friends reassured each other, and most of the upperclassmen, like me, just smiled and changed. This time, when I walked into the locker room, everything got quiet.

***

Read the alternate ending

Read Skye's story!

Chasing Skye

ALSO BY KELSIE STELTING

The Curvy Girl Club

Curvy Girls Can't Date Quarterbacks

Curvy Girls Can't Date Billionaires

Curvy Girls Can't Date Cowboys

Curvy Girls Can't Date Bad Boys

Curvy Girls Can't Date Best Friends

Curvy Girls Can't Date Bullies

Curvy Girls Can't Dance

Curvy Girls Can't Date Soldiers

Curvy Girls Can't Date Princes

Curvy Girls Can't Date Rock Stars

Curvy Girls Can't Date Surfers

Curvy Girls Can't Date Curvy Girls (Pride Edition)

The Texas High Series

Chasing Skye

Becoming Skye

Loving Skye

Always Anika

New at Texas High

Abi and the Boy Next Door

Abi and the Boy Who Lied

Abi and the Boy She Loves

The Pen Pal Romance Series

Dear Adam

Fabio Vs. the Friend Zone

Sincerely Cinderella

Standalone YA Romance

Road Trip with the Enemy

YA Contemporary Romance Anthologies

The Art of Taking Chances

Two More Days

Nonfiction

Raising the West

ACKNOWLEDGMENTS

My deepest gratitude goes to Ty Stelting, Jennifer Hoss, Autumn Mays, Carol Bussen, Angie Goudy, and Melanie Bergeron for their commentary on *Always Anika*.

To my editors, Melanie Bergeron and Theresa Cole, thank you for helping *Always Anika* reach its full potential!

I exist as an author because of readers like yourself, and your support means the world to me. Thank you times a million for spending time with me in this story and along my writing journey.

AUTHOR'S NOTE

Thank you for reading *Always Anika*! I hope you enjoyed Anika's story and her little corner of Texas. I started writing *Always Anika* as a sophomore in high school. Back then, there was an app on Facebook called "Bathroom Wall," and tons of kids from all over would post segments of stories as serials. As often as I could, I would write little bits of Anika's story and eagerly read all of the comments people left. Imagine a facebook post with the first paragraph of the story, and the rest posted in the comments and you would have something similar to Bathroom Wall. It was truly one of the best author communities I have ever been a part of and it proved a few things to me that I appreciate more now that I'm a little older.

I learned that people love good stories. There's this myth out there that people don't like to read anymore, but that's what a bunch of kids did with their free time on BW. We wrote and we read and we were always on the lookout for the next great story. Another thing I learned was that you don't have to be a bestseller to write good stories that people love to read.

My stories might not be the greatest literary works of all time, but they follow real people through real life. No, Anika isn't an actual person, but I think a lot of us can identify with heartbreak, with hope, with having to make a hard decision that may or may not work out. While we read, we aren't just students putting off homework; we're receiving letters from a dreamboat named Shawn Adams, we're going on late-night horseback rides with Kyle Rayford, and we're riding home from school with Bran.

I picked back up and began editing it when my brother was in the hospital. *Always Anika* was my escape when real life was too difficult to bear.

Maybe Anika didn't always have her act together. But neither do the rest of us. What we all have in common, is that we can always be ourselves, and that is always good enough.

ABOUT THE AUTHOR

Kelsie Stelting is a body positive romance author who writes love stories with strong characters, deep feelings, and happy endings.

She currently lives in Colorado with her family. You can often find her writing, spending time with family, and soaking up too much sun wherever she can find it.

Visit www.kelsiestelting.com to get a free story and sign up for her readers' group!

Made in United States
North Haven, CT
13 August 2024